WILD L.A.

TYSON WILD BOOK SIXTEEN

TRIPP ELLIS

D0888729

TRIPP ELLIS

WELCOME

Want more books like this?

You'll probably never hear about my new releases unless you join my newsletter.

SIGN UP HERE

1

—————

*The names and locations have been fictionalized to protect the
innocent and the guilty...*

It was probably a bad idea, but when JD gets an idea in
his head, there's no stopping him.

Diver Down had always been a low-key, family-
friendly type of venue. Sure it got a little out of hand during
spring break, but otherwise, it was generally pretty tame. JD
wanted to throw an all-out bash for Independence Day,
complete with a homemade bikini contest.

Against my better judgment, I let him run the show.

I had to admit, he was a damn good organizer. He had
planned everything down to the smallest detail. Nothing
was left to chance. During the process, he had a perpetual
grin on his face. Jack Donovan liked to party, and no
expense was spared.

A temporary stage was built on the outdoor patio with a short runway that allowed the girls to prance the catwalk. Jack had arranged for a misting station to be built. It was an archway over the catwalk that drizzled the girls as they strutted down the stage. The fine mist mixed with their oiled skin creating delightfully glistening curves. Water beaded on toned, tanned bodies—flat stomachs, ample bosoms, tight tushies. The taut fabric grew damp and revealing. The peaks and valleys inspired lustful fantasies. Music pumped through massive speakers as a DJ spun tunes while the girls showed off their creativity.

I had to give it to Jack. This was a hell of a bikini contest. Perhaps the best I'd ever seen. The talent was strong. More than strong. Phenomenal. The judges would have a difficult time.

Some of the girls were actual designers and had fabricated elegant, revealing swimsuits. Made from the finest fabric, and stitched to perfection, these would-be fashion mavens were hoping the bikini contest might be a springboard to launching their designs, boosting sales from their websites.

Others had less lofty aspirations.

They were just trying to make the most revealing outfit possible, relying on their natural gifts to win the judges over.

And there were plenty of natural gifts.

A wardrobe malfunction was an ever-present threat. One that was most welcomed by the judges and the crowd.

There were bikinis made from duct tape, bumper stickers,

trash bags, cellophane, red plastic beer cups, leather hide, rose petals strategically glued in place, and dental floss.

As each new contestant bobbled and jiggled her way down the stage, the crowd went wild. There were howls, whistles, and catcalls. Drunk men practically drooled on themselves.

Jack had convinced *Coconut Cream Sunscreen* to put up a cash prize of $10,000.

The girls pulled out all the stops.

Diver Down smelled like a combination of beer, whiskey, and coconut oil. Piña coladas and strawberry daiquiris dangled from inebriated hands.

Many of the girls decided to demonstrate how easy it was to remove some of their homemade wares, eliciting more wild cheers from the crowd. The girls bounced and undulated, their slick, glistening curves on full display. Wide eyes from the crowd ogled the sumptuous delights.

A DJ with a low, smooth voice announced each of the girls as they took the stage. Many of them worked at *Forbidden Fruit*, the infamous strip club on Oyster Avenue. They were no stranger to bearing all for lecherous crowds.

Jack's band, *Wild Fury*, was set to play after the bikini contest. After that, a barrage of fireworks would dazzle the crowd with a colorful display of pyrotechnics. It was THE place to be on Coconut Key.

Jack and I stood by the stage during the contest. JD grinned with pride at his accomplishment.

Several of the offstage contestants hung around JD, pawing

at him, hoping to curry favor. Jack wasn't judging the competition and had no say in the matter, but he didn't seem to mind the bevy of hotties that surrounded him.

That was until Sloan arrived.

"Am I catching you at a bad time?" she asked with an arched eyebrow.

"Oh, no! Not at all," Jack said, trying not to look guilty.

He slipped away from the beauties and stepped toward Sloan. Pouty looks twisted the bikini models' faces.

JD was smitten with the sultry brunette, and it was easy to see why. Sloan was smart, witty, and had a successful career as a pro golfer. She could see right through JD's bullshit. That made her all the more alluring to him, I'm sure. Her gorgeous blue eyes, sculpted cheekbones, pillowy lips, and toned body didn't hurt either.

The two hadn't officially been on a *date* yet, but this was the second time she had ventured out to see JD's band play. At this point, he hadn't even gotten to first base.

There must have been *some* interest on her part. Why else would she keep accepting his invitations?

"Can I get you a drink?" JD asked.

"Sure," Sloan said, then eyed the bikini-clad beauties by the stage. "I don't want to pull you away from your entourage."

She tried to sound disinterested, but underneath the slightly sardonic tone in her voice, the glimmer in her eyes betrayed her amusement—JD had abandoned the other temptations. And Sloan liked it.

"I'm sure I can slip away for a few moments."

JD offered his arm, and Sloan accepted.

Sloan muttered to me, "Eden broke up with her boyfriend."

That caught my attention. "Good to know. Where is she? Why didn't you bring her along?"

Sloan's friend Eden was a gorgeous blonde, also on the Pro tour.

"She's out of town."

"Well, maybe we could all go on a double date when she gets back?" I suggested.

A hopeful smile flashed on JD's face.

"Better strike while the iron is hot. She won't be off the market for long," Sloan said.

"I imagine not," I replied.

JD led Sloan to the bar, and she ordered a strawberry daiquiri.

I watched the rest of the bikini contest while JD tried to reel Sloan in. He had her on the hook, but one wrong move and this one could get away.

My phone buzzed my pocket with a call from Sheriff Daniels. I swiped the screen and put the device to my ear. "I just gotta warn you, it's my day off. I'm overseeing a massive party at the bar. And I'm leaving town tomorrow. So whatever it is you're about to tell me, I don't want to know."

"You're leaving town tomorrow?" Daniels asked.

"Yes. I told you that last week."

Daniels grumbled to himself, remembering my advanced notice. "Well, I think you'll want to hear this, anyway. But if you're too busy, I'll just tell you when you get back."

2

___

"**D**alton Lennox escaped," Daniels said in a grim tone.

"What!?" I exclaimed. "How?"

Lennox was a ruthless serial killer that had a penchant for carving up young girls. His killing spree had started in Boston, and continued through New York. From there, he headed south and dabbled in the Carolinas, then went hog-wild in Florida.

He'd been locked up for the last half-dozen years, well before I arrived back in Coconut Key. The notorious killer had managed to capture national attention due to the grisly nature of his crimes, contrasted by his pleasant demeanor and good looks. He always seemed quite charming in interviews and had no shortage of female fans. The dark-haired butcher had a square jaw, dark eyes, and a vile and depraved heart. The Harvard educated, former doctor, was a force to be reckoned with—smart, capable, and cunning.

"Prisoner transfer," Daniels continued. "A correctional

officer at CCCI was taking him up to Raiford when some jackass ran a red light and T-boned the patrol car. Spun the vehicle around, knocking the officer unconscious. Dalton kicked out the back window and took off on foot."

"How's the officer?"

"He's okay. Concussion, broken leg. He's in the hospital now. I've got a BOLO out on Lennox."

"He can't get too far," I said.

"Don't count on it." Daniels sighed. "The last thing we need is a scumbag like that roaming the streets. But, since you're leaving town, it's not your problem."

"I'll be back in a few days."

"I'm sure we'll have Lennox under wraps by then," Daniels said. "Highway Patrol's got a checkpoint set up, and I've got eyes in the sky."

"If it were me, I wouldn't try to get off the island on the highway. Too risky."

"What would you do?"

"The first thing I'd do is get out of that orange jumpsuit, get those handcuffs off, and get out of the search grid."

"He managed to snatch the officer's keys. I'm assuming he's out of the cuffs."

"Any eyewitnesses?"

"Several. He was last seen running south down Hampton Street. Faulkner and Erickson are canvassing the area now along with several other deputies."

"Check the marinas. I'd steal a boat and head to Cuba."

"I'll notify the Coast Guard," Daniels said.

"Keep me posted."

"I will." In a dry tone, Daniels said, "Enjoy your trip."

I ended the call and slipped the phone into my pocket.

Dalton Lennox was not a guy you wanted running around on the streets. The thought of him loose in Coconut Key gnawed at me.

I moved to the bar and ordered a beer from Alejandro. He had hired on a few temp bartenders for the festivities. Teagan was still taking time off, recovering from her injuries. I wasn't sure she would ever come back after what had happened. I wouldn't blame her if she didn't.

Alejandro pulled a bottle opener from his pocket, twirled it, and popped the top. Air hissed, and he slid the sweaty bottle across the counter to me. I gave a nod of appreciation, then took a sip of the cold brew from the amber longneck.

I glanced down the bar. JD and Sloan seemed like they were getting along well. She was laughing and smiling at his jokes, flicking her hair, batting her eyelashes. She had inched closer to him. Maybe the old *Donovan Charm* was working on her?

The bikini contest was winding down. The last contestant strutted the catwalk.

"Can you handle the rest of the contest for me?" JD asked.

He didn't want to break away from Sloan.

I nodded and headed toward the stage. The DJ's low voice

rumbled through the PA speakers. "Let's give a warm round of applause for our contestants."

There were hoots and hollers and claps.

"The judges will confer, and we will have our winner shortly," the DJ said.

The judges took a few minutes to tally their scores, making painstaking calculations. Their faces twisted with agony as they debated whom to award the $10,000 prize.

All the girls were winners, but there could be only one.

Once the judges tabulated the results, they handed the scores to me, and I made my way to the stage. I grabbed the owner of *Coconut Cream Sunscreen,* Tristan, and he followed me to the stage, holding a giant check for $10,000.

The wireless microphone squealed as I first turned it on, then the feedback faded. "Was that talent, or was that talent?"

The audience roared.

"I'm so glad that I'm not a judge," I continued. "Before we go any further, I'd like to thank all of the contestants for their hard work and design skills."

The crowd whistled and hooted.

"Let's give a big round of applause to our sponsor, *Coconut Cream Sunscreen*. All day, waterproof protection that doesn't leave you feeling greasy."

The owner bowed and waved to the crowd.

"I've been told that, right now, all *Coconut Cream Sunscreen* products are on sale via their website with a special discount code of ID4BIKINI."

The crowd didn't care about the sunscreen. They were just here for the girls.

"Without any further ado, let's get to the results."

The raucous crowd cheered.

I looked over the results, paused for dramatic effect, then, in my best announcer voice, said, "The third runner-up is Brittany Miles!"

The crowd howled.

Brittany bounced up and down and strutted to the stage like she'd just won the lottery.

Tristan's assistant handed her a gift basket of various sunscreens, moisturizers, and beauty products.

"The second runner-up is Carolina Cole!" I shouted.

She was a beautiful blonde with an infectious smile. She made her way to the stage, pranced down the runway and back one last time, soaking in the adulation of the crowd.

Tristan's assistant handed her a similar gift basket. Carolina smiled and waved to the crowd before taking her place next to Brittany.

"The first runner-up is Sabrina Talbot," I announced.

The gorgeous brunette shrieked with joy. She bobbled to the stage, took her congratulatory walk, and received another gift basket.

"And the moment you've all been waiting for... the grand

prize winner... and the inaugural *Miss Diver Down,* Sierra Peaks!"

Sierra bounced up and down, covering her mouth as she almost burst into tears. She pulled herself together, climbed to the stage, and strutted down the catwalk, waving to the crowd. She fanned her eyes as she teared up.

Tristan handed her the giant check, and the two stood together for publicity photos.

"Congratulations, Sierra!" I said. "Can you tell us about what inspired your design?"

She took the microphone. "As you can see, I'm wearing dental floss."

There were more howls from the crowd.

She'd actually taken the time to weave the dental floss into a pattern that resembled a bikini—a very teeny tiny bikini. One that covered little more than pasties would. And down below, it barely covered the promised land. There was a small little landing strip visible that pointed the way.

It was hard not to become enamored with her design. Her slick body glistened in the sunlight.

"I'm sure you have a bright future in the bikini world," I said.

Sierra smiled. "I sure hope so. Be sure to visit my website." She gave the horde her web address.

The crowd cheered again, and we all left the stage.

Sierra posed for more photos with the giant check and Tristan.

The DJ spun tunes, and the inebriated crowd drifted from the stage to refill their beverages and take a much-needed pitstop.

After all the photos were taken, and the camera flashes had stopped, Sierra sauntered in my direction. The dental floss bikini struggled to maintain its form. It was hard not to ogle the design, but then again, that's what it was designed for.

"I just wanted to say thank you for giving me this opportunity," Sierra said.

"Don't thank me, thank JD. This was all his idea." I pointed across the bar to Jack.

"He looks kind of preoccupied at the moment," Sierra said.

"Indeed."

"Well, I'm sure you will pass along my gratitude."

"I will."

"Will you be having another contest next year?"

"This was such a hit, I imagine we would have to." I smiled.

"Yay!" Her joy quickly turned to a frown. "You won't disqualify previous winners, will you?"

"Actually, I haven't given a lot of thought to the rules."

She smiled. "Well, I think it would be great if you let reigning champions compete."

"I will have to keep that in consideration," I said.

She smiled, and her blue eyes glimmered. When the light hit her auburn hair, you could see the deep red in it. "What was your name again?"

"Tyson Wild."

We shook hands.

Her eyes narrowed with recognition. "You're that guy. That cop. I've seen you on TV. You dated Bree Taylor."

I nodded. "Briefly."

"Such a shame what happened to her. She seemed like such a sweetheart."

"She was."

She frowned. "I'm sorry." Sierra sighed. "Well, I guess I should let you get back to whatever it was you were doing."

She lingered with a devious sparkle in her eyes. I think she was hoping I would keep my attention focused on her. At the moment, I couldn't think of a better place to focus it.

"I'm not particularly busy at the moment," I said. "Can I get you a drink?"

"I really should get out of this swimsuit and into something less revealing."

I looked over her makeshift bikini one more time. With a straight face, I said, "I don't see anything revealing about this."

She chuckled. "This outfit doesn't leave me with any secrets."

"I don't think you have anything to hide."

"How about I go get changed, then I'll come find you for that drink?"

"I believe that sounds acceptable."

She smiled, spun around, and sauntered toward the side of the stage where she had left a duffel bag with her clothing. From there, she headed to the women's restroom.

I made my way back to the bar and waited for my new drinking buddy.

3

Sierra joined me at the bar for a piña colada. The outfit she changed into wasn't as revealing as the dental floss bikini, but it was still pretty slim on fabric. She wore a cream-colored bikini top that accented her tanned skin. The seams of the taut garment screamed for mercy, struggling to contain her prize-winning peaks. She wore a cream sheer sarong around her waist that acted like a flowing skirt.

She looked good. Damn good!

"Is that one of your designs?" I asked.

She smiled, and her pearly teeth glimmered. "It is. You like?"

"I do. It's a little more substantial than the dental floss."

"So, are you saying you'd like to see less of me?" There was a naughty glimmer in her eyes.

"Quite the contrary," I said. "The dental floss certainly had its charm."

She giggled.

I introduced her to JD and Sloan.

"This was all his idea," I said.

"So, I have you to thank for my $10,000 check?" Sierra asked, playfully.

"And you deserve every penny," JD said.

Sloan rolled her eyes.

JD gave Sloan an innocent look and shrugged.

"Sierra designs a line of swimwear," I said.

"And lingerie," she added. "I'm entering as many of these bikini contests as I can, hoping it will be a springboard for my designs. It's good marketing."

"You know, Tyson and I are accomplished photographers. We do a lot of model photoshoots. We're the official photographers of Coconut Cream Sunscreen." JD couldn't help himself.

Sierra lifted an impressed eyebrow. "Is that so? I need better photography. What I've got on the website doesn't really showcase my designs to their fullest."

"We'd be happy to help," JD said.

"That's fantastic. What would you charge? I don't have a lot of money right now."

"You just won $10k!" JD exclaimed, incredulous.

"This venture isn't generating a ton of revenue at this point. I'm dancing over at *Forbidden Fruit* to support this whole endeavor. I plan on dumping the $10K into manufacturing and, of course, marketing, but that doesn't go very far. This whole *entrepreneur thing* is expensive."

"Tyson is the finance manager," JD said. "I'm sure you can work out something with him."

Her eyes sparkled. "I'm sure we can."

Sloan watched with amusement.

JD had thrown the ball into my court, trying not to look too eager to fill the boat with bikini-clad hotties. I didn't figure Sloan for the jealous type, but she certainly enjoyed watching JD squirm as he fought against his natural inclination to surround himself with beautiful women.

JD tried to twist the situation to his advantage. "Maybe you could do me a favor," he said to Sierra.

She arched an intrigued eyebrow.

"I've been trying to get this one to go on a date with me," JD said, nodding to Sloan. "But she says she'll only go with a chaperone. Apparently, she doesn't trust me."

"Is that what I said?" Sloan muttered dryly.

"If you agree to go on a date with Tyson, we could all double, and through peer pressure, Sloan would have to agree to go on the date."

"Would I?" she asked with a playfully skeptical tone.

"Yes, you would," JD answered with a smile.

Sierra pondered the situation. "I guess I could consent to something like that."

A wide smile curled JD's face. "It's settled then. We're all going on a double date. How's tomorrow night sound?"

"No can do. LA tomorrow, remember?" I said.

"Sorry," Sloan said. "I have a tournament next week. Leaving town tomorrow as well."

JD frowned.

"But, I could be talked into it when I get back," Sloan added.

"I will most certainly take a rain check." JD was on cloud nine.

Sierra finished her piña colada. "I hate to win the contest and run, but I need to go."

I frowned. "You're not staying for the fireworks?"

"I'd love to stay for the fireworks, but it's my grandmother's birthday. I told her I would swing by the assisted living facility after the contest and make sure she got to see some fireworks."

"You can bring her back here," I suggested.

She looked around the venue. "I think this isn't quite her style right now. A little too crowded."

"Understood."

"But I'll be looking forward to that double," Sierra said with an optimistic smile. "Give me your phone."

I handed the device to her, and she programmed in her number.

"Don't be afraid to use it." She gave me a kiss on the cheek before leaving. "Thanks for the drink."

"Anytime." I watched her gather her things and saunter out of the bar.

"I've gotta hand it to you," Sloan said. "You two are slick. Real slick."

We both played innocent.

Sloan arched a skeptical eyebrow at JD and muttered to herself, "What have I gotten myself into?"

4

J
D's band took the stage in the late afternoon. He had changed out of his traditional outfit—Hawaiian shirt and cargo shorts—and into his rock 'n' roll attire. JD assumed his stage persona, *Thrash*.

He had a red bandana around his forehead, and his long blonde hair flowed past his shoulders. He wore leather pants, a leather vest over a concert T-shirt, skull rings on his fingers, studded bracelets, and eyeliner.

Sloan chuckled with amusement at his getup.

Styxx took his place behind a candy-apple red drum set, and Crash plucked a groovy baseline. It was in perfect time with the kick drum and the ticking of a high-hat. Dizzy riffed on guitar, buzzing like a chainsaw. The wall of sound washed over the crowd, and JD howled into the microphone, "Are you ready to rock 'n' roll?"

The crowd went crazy.

JD's tribute band was a spot-on, time capsule replica of a

beloved '80s hair-metal band. They pounded out a setlist that kept the audience craving more, throwing in a few of their original compositions along the way.

A horde of the band's regular groupies swarmed the venue. There was a lot of teased hair, heavy eyeliner, and fishnet stockings. *Diver Down* turned into an odd mix of metal-heads, beach bums, sun-seekers, college kids, and regulars.

Sloan stayed for the whole show.

Afterward, JD and company left the stage amid a sea of adoring groupies.

Jack usually reveled in the attention, but it was easy to see that someone else was on his mind. He signed a few autographs, then escaped his fan club to rejoin with Sloan.

He was a love-sick puppy dog.

"What did you think?" JD asked.

Sloan shrugged, feigning disappointment for a brief moment. Then she smiled. "I gotta admit. It's growing on me. Like a fungus. But it's growing on me, nonetheless."

JD scowled at her playfully.

Sloan finally came clean. "It was good. I mean, it's not totally my type of music. But you guys are tight. And, if I'm being honest, I like your original songs better."

A prideful grin curled on JD's face. "I'm kind of partial to those myself. Who knows? Maybe one of these days, that's all we'll play?"

"It seems like you've got a growing fan base."

A blonde with teased hair dragged her brunette friend to JD.

She wore a low-cut top, revealing ample endowments. She arched out her chest, practically sticking her boobs in JD's face. "Would you sign these for me?"

Jack's eyes were drawn to the voluptuous mounds. He swallowed hard, then looked hesitantly to Sloan. "Um, sure."

Jack prepared to sign both of the girls' bosoms with a black sharpie. He looked for the best surface to write on, and the best angle to approach it from, studying the mounds carefully. With Jack's resemblance to the famous '80s singer, it was hard to tell if they were genuinely asking for his autograph, or the celebrity's?

With a delicate touch, Jack started to sign the women's breasts.

"Don't be shy. You can touch them as much as you want," the blonde said.

JD cupped her boob, creating a stable writing platform.

Sloan seemed amused.

With Jack's signature complete, the girls bounced up and down with excitement and gave JD a hug, then flitted off.

JD shrugged. "Gotta give the fans what they want."

Sloan rolled her eyes.

The sun had settled over the horizon, and it wasn't long before fireworks exploded in the night sky. The dazzling pyrotechnics sparkled with colorful hues of red, blue, and white. Deafening explosions thundered, rattling my chest. The rockets' red glare reflected across the water. Colorful bursts were followed by pops and crackles. Smoke drifted with the breeze. There were *oohs* and *ahhhs* from the crowd as they were awed by the glorious display.

JD put his arm around Sloan, and she didn't remove it.

After the show, the crowd thinned slightly, but the bar was still pretty packed. The rest of the band—Crash, Dizzy, and Styxx—drank their fill at the bar.

At the end of the night, Sloan gave JD a peck on the cheek before leaving. He seemed delighted. He practically skipped toward me afterward. "Did you see that?"

"I did."

"My plan is working."

"She's a nice girl. I like her."

"That's number seven right there."

My brow lifted with surprise. "What!?"

Jack smiled.

"Have you lost your mind? You barely know each other."

"I got a good feeling about this one."

"I'm sure you had a good feeling about the other six, too." Jack went through wives faster than most people traded in cars. It was an expensive hobby.

He frowned at me. "Yeah, but that was different. I was going into those for the wrong reasons."

I shook my head. "Just take it easy."

"Oh, don't worry, I'm all about easy. I'm just saying, I think she's the one. I could be wrong, but I got this funny feeling inside."

"That's called lust."

"I think, by this point in time, I know the difference."

I raised my hands in surrender.

JD hesitated, then sheepishly said, "So, I'm not going to fly out to Los Angeles with you tomorrow."

I raised a curious eyebrow. "What about your show?"

"We're still playing *Sour Mash* Friday night. I'll fly out later tomorrow or the next day. Sloan said she'd have lunch with me tomorrow, and I promised to take her to the airport in the afternoon."

"Um, okay. Whatever you want to do."

"The band is going to drive the gear out to Cali in the van. I could use a little more time to help them load up and prep everything for the show, anyway," JD said, making excuses.

"You don't need to explain anything to me," I said, trying not to harass him too much.

JD hung around the bar for the rest of the night, talking incessantly about how amazing Sloan was and how well they clicked. I was happy for him, I really was. But it was starting to get nauseating.

The bar closed at 2 AM, and I helped Alejandro and the staff clean up after the event. When the chairs were stacked atop tables, and everything wiped down, I ambled to the *Vivere* and packed a bag for the morning.

Teagan said she would look after the animals. I had dropped

them at her apartment before the festivities. She was getting along well but wasn't quite up to standing behind the bar all day. She said the little fur-babies would keep her company and lift her spirits while she recovered.

The last thing she had said to me as I was leaving her apartment was, "Be careful out there. I don't mean to freak you out, but I've got a bad feeling."

I had assured her that everything would be okay. Whether she was truly psychic, I couldn't say. But I knew when Teagan issued a warning, it was worth heeding.

5

W*hat could go wrong?*

The ominous thought cycled through my brain as I boarded the *G750 Slipstream* aircraft. The private jet was the epitome of luxury. Sleek, modern lines. Plush beige seats that fully reclined. Polished wood trim, surround sound stereo, flatscreen displays, and an accommodating staff.

"Can I get you something to drink, Mr. Wild?" a gorgeous flight attendant asked, a shimmering river of blonde hair dangling around her shoulders.

I smiled. "Bottled water, please."

"Right away, sir."

It wasn't my jet, but the studio gave me access every time I needed to travel to Los Angeles on official business.

I buckled my safety harness, reclined my seat, and tried not to think about Teagan's warning. It could have been in reference to anything. Was there a mechanical fault with the plane? Was it going to crash? Was something terrible going to happen when I was in Los Angeles?

I dismissed it and gave it no more credence than I would any other word of caution coming from a friend. Though Teagan was often right when it came to predicting future events.

The pilot's voice crackled over the intercom. He announced our flight time and urged me to "Sit back, relax, and enjoy the flight."

The engines whined, and the aircraft raced down the tarmac. The fuselage rattled, and the acceleration forced me back into the seat. The nose lifted, and we gently glided into the air. A moment later, the wheels retracted, and we angled toward the sky.

The flight attendant brought me a bottle of water after we had leveled off.

"My name is Cassandra. Let me know if there's anything else I can get for you."

There was a delicious sparkle in her blue eyes, and she seemed eager to please. I wondered how eager?

With the time change, the flight would put me into the FBO at Burbank at a little after 11:30 AM, Pacific time. I had a little over five hours to kill.

I think Cassandra was a little bored because she checked on me again in 15 minutes. "I have breakfast tacos if you would like some. And for lunch, you have the option of meatloaf, chicken Parmesan, or a chicken salad."

"Breakfast tacos sound good. In a few hours, I think I'll take the chicken salad."

Cassandra smiled. "Excellent choice. I also have beer, wine, and cocktails."

"It's probably a little early for that."

"It's 5 o'clock somewhere."

"Look at you trying to be a bad influence."

"I'm just here to serve," she said, not sounding so innocent.

She certainly looked enticing in that tight uniform, the short skirt hugging her hips.

"Did you have a good 4th of July?" Cassandra asked.

"I did. You?"

"I had a layover in Coconut Key. So, I went to Oyster Avenue with some girlfriends, watched the fireworks, and had a good time."

"Are you based out of LA?"

She nodded.

"Do you fly strictly for the studio?"

"Yes. The studio has an exclusive charter with us, and we take their clients all over the world."

"I bet you've met some pretty famous people."

"I have. It's an interesting job. Most of the people are really cool."

"I'm sure there have been some real jackasses, too."

Her subtle smirk said everything. "Your words, not mine."

"Don't worry, I won't give you much trouble."

"I had you pegged as one of the good guys from the moment you stepped aboard. But trouble... you look like a handful.“

"And what makes you say that?"

"Just a hunch. Am I wrong?" she asked with a flirty glance.

"I'm an evil villain, watch out!"

She laughed.

“So, what's your evil plan? World domination?”

“Something like that.”

“Need a sidekick?”

“Maybe.”

“Wait, no! Villains don't have sidekicks. They have hench-men. You need a hench-woman.”

“What's your superpower?”

A devious smirk curled on her full lips. “You'll have to discover that for yourself.”

We entertained each other for most of the flight. When we landed, she gave me her number and said to call if I wanted someone to show me around LA. I'm sure she could show me a few places I hadn't seen before.

The studio sent a limousine to pick me up from the airport. The driver met me on the tarmac, holding a sign that read: *Wild*. He introduced himself, grabbed my bag, and escorted me to the car. He got the door as I slid into the comfy leather seats, then loaded my bag into the trunk.

Nash was his name—a different driver than last time, but equally as cordial. He chauffeured me through the city, over the hill, down Highland, and west on Sunset Boulevard. The route had become familiar, and it almost felt like coming to a home away from home. Massive billboards with movie posters towered over the avenue. There were blockbuster advertisements on the sides of buses and a constant bustle of foot traffic on the sidewalks.

I had to admit, the star treatment didn't suck.

After a short drive, we pulled into the *Château Montmar*. Nash hopped out of the car and pulled open my door. He snatched my bag from the trunk, and I told him I could handle it from there. I put $20 in his hand, and he nodded with appreciation. He gave me his card and told me to call if I needed a ride anywhere.

"Welcome back, Mr. Wild," the desk clerk said as I stepped to the counter.

After a few keystrokes, I was handed keys, and a bellhop escorted me to my room. He showed me about the suite, and I placed a tip in the bellhop's palm. With that, he was gone.

I had the room to myself.

The old hotel was full of stories, and the walls kept their secrets well. The accommodations were nice, but not opulent. I guess that was part of its old-world charm. It was a castle perched at the foot of the Hollywood Hills, ensconced by trees. A monument to Hollywood excess.

Full of scandal and history, it exuded glamour and depravity at the same time—an enigmatic presence that was almost alive. A place where you could lose or find yourself. Another world where the conventional rules didn't seem to apply. The lure of pleasure and sinful delights beckoned.

LA was the type of place where everything could be had for a price. And people would sell their soul just to pay the rent. Anything for a chance to stay one more day in the city of infinite possibilities. One more day to step through the looking glass. A city full of hopes and dreams, which often ended as broken nightmares.

What happened at the Château, stayed at the Château.

My suite had two bedrooms, a living area, a kitchen, and a small office space. A cozy crib, suitable for a brief stay, or an extended escape that could last weeks or months—if you could pay the bill.

On the desk was a stack of personalized stationery.

I called my agent, Joel, and let him know that I was in town.

"Excellent. I take it you had a good flight?"

"I'm alive and in one piece."

"Always a plus. David's already checked into the Château. He wants to sequester in for as long as it takes to get the first season of episodes outlined."

As nice as the hotel was, I didn't want to be cooped up for days on end.

"Whenever you're settled in, give him a call, and you two can agree on a schedule. Keep me posted."

I ended the call. Before I rang David, I called Tracy Thomas and let her know that I had arrived in Los Angeles. I told her I would look into her daughter's case as time permitted.

Part of me thought I would come to the conclusion that Mia Sophia's death was due to the excesses of a young starlet. But there was that voice in the back of my mind that said there was something more.

From my hotel room, I could see the pool below where Mia Sophia had died. If only these walls could talk.

6

"Margot Wade," Tracy said, her voice crackling through the speaker on my phone. "That's who you need to talk to. She was friends with Mia in high school. That's who Mia stayed with when she first moved to Los Angeles."

"Have you spoken with her?" I asked.

"Briefly. She didn't have much to say. She was in a rush, heading out to an audition. Said she hadn't seen Mia in a long time. I got the sense that there was something she wasn't telling me. But maybe that's just my overactive imagination."

"Do you have a phone number and an address for her?" I asked.

"Yeah. I'll text you after we hang up." She paused. "Also, the reporter. The one who got the autopsy report that I sent you. Lyric Stone. You might want to talk to her. She sounds like a real go-getter."

"I'll let you know what I find out."

Tracy thanked me again for taking a look into the case before I ended the call.

I glanced at the time. I had arranged to meet David Cameron in the bar shortly. I figured I'd give Margot a call after my meeting with David.

I left my room and headed down to the bar. It wasn't nearly as crowded as it would get in the evenings, but there were still quite a few people in the establishment. It was a typical Hollywood scene—people enjoying expensive happy hour drinks, closing deals, pitching projects. You couldn't take a step in Los Angeles without tripping over the business. It was everywhere. Everyone had a story to tell, a project to hustle, a dream to fulfill.

At night, the bar was more seductive and alluring. More mystical. During the day, it seemed less mysterious.

I scanned the secluded booths, the deep couches, the oak bar—David hadn't arrived yet.

I made my way to the bar and leaned against the counter. It didn't take long to get the bartender's attention. I flashed my badge quickly. I had no jurisdiction here, but the flicker of a shiny gold shield usually got people's attention. Most of the time they didn't really bother to look at it.

I surveyed the bartender carefully, trying to place his face in my memory, but he didn't look familiar. "You weren't here the night Mia Sophia passed, were you?"

He shook his head. "No. I was off that night."

He wore a white shirt, black vest, and black tie. He had

blond hair, blue eyes, and chiseled features. Probably a model or an actor looking to catch a break, paying the bills in the meantime by slinging drinks.

"You want to talk to Marcel," he continued.

"Is he around?"

"No. I think he's in tomorrow evening."

I felt a hand on my shoulder and turned to see David's smiling face. We shook hands.

"Good to see you, buddy," David said.

"And you. You're looking well."

"I feel great," David said, exuberant. "Not bad for a guy who was at death's door."

I had to agree. There didn't seem to be any residual effects from the accident.

David was in his mid-30s, had brown hair, and a well-trimmed goatee. He was dressed in jeans and a black T-shirt. The guy had been responsible for a few of the highest-grossing franchises of all time. He was surprisingly down to earth and devoid of any ego. From what I had observed in my dealings with him, he didn't fall into the trappings of Hollywood. He seemed to have a true passion for the work and a commitment to telling stories that took audiences on an enjoyable ride.

David motioned to a secluded booth. "Let's grab a seat."

We drifted through the dim bar and slid into a curved leather booth with a deep-buttoned Chesterfield-style cushion on the back.

"What was it like?" David asked, leaning into the table, whispering.

"What was *what* like?"

"You know, dying?"

I took a deep breath, not sure how much detail I wanted to go into about my near death experience. "It wasn't pleasant, let's put it that way."

"Did you see the other side?"

I shrugged. "I was a traveler on a journey to an unknown destination. A destination I didn't necessarily want to be at, if you get my drift."

A wave of recognition flashed in David's eyes.

"It was as real as anything I had ever experienced."

"So, you went to the *other* place," David said, curious.

I nodded.

"But yet you're back. You got a second chance."

"Indeed. And I intend to make the most of it."

The wheels turned behind David's eyes.

"What about you?" I asked, turning the tables.

"When I was in a coma? I felt like I was hanging on between here and there. A weird dreamland. I can't make much sense of it. But I felt like I was given the choice to stay or go. And I remember saying I'm not ready to go yet. Though, it didn't seem like a bad place to go."

"Lucky for you," I said.

"You seem like a decent guy, Tyson. I'm curious as to why you would go to the *other* place."

I forced a smile. "I guess it's just my charming personality."

David chuckled. "You'll have to be more forthcoming than that. We're developing a TV show, after all. We need drama and intrigue. Danger and excitement. Love and loss."

"Don't worry. There's plenty of that."

He chuckled again. "If you haven't gathered, I'm a very intense and focused guy. Over the next few days, I want to devote all of my energy to mapping out the basic series arc. From there, we'll give the outline to the writers, and they will craft the episodes. I consider you a friend, Tyson. And by the end of this process, I hope we both will have a deeper understanding of one another. And hopefully, we won't want to kill each other."

I laughed. "It's just a TV show."

"Yes, but I'm passionate about everything I do. And I have a feeling you're the same way. Though, something tells me your passions are quite a bit more violent than mine. I just fantasize about car chases and helicopters exploding. Chasing down bad guys and saving the world. You actually do those things."

I feigned modesty. "From time to time."

"I figured we could lock ourselves in a hotel room, do a bunch of cocaine, and knock this thing out in no time."

I gave him a look.

"I'm kidding about the cocaine. But there's no law against overdosing on coffee."

We shared a laugh.

"How do we start?" I asked. "For the Bree Taylor project, I just told my story, and the writer turned it into something that was a reasonable facsimile of reality."

"I need to absorb the information. I think we should have a few drinks and you just tell me stories. From there, I'll start breaking the ideas down into episodes, and create an overall season arc." David smiled. "Trust me. It's not going to feel like work. This is the fun part. The idea stage. It's not the *brain-bleed* stage."

"What's the *brain-bleed* stage?" I asked with concern.

"That's when you stare at a blank page and you have to make sense of all your notes."

We laughed again.

A cute waitress in a white blouse and black skirt swung by the table and took our drink order.

I began to regale David with wild tales of adventure. Most of them true.

7

We drank into the night, shot the shit, and had a good time. It didn't seem like work at all. It was hard to believe I was getting paid millions for this. But, as David said, this was the easy part. Fortunately, I didn't have to deal with the hard part. I'd been keeping a daily journal, but that wasn't for public consumption.

After the sun went down, the bar filled, and the volume rose. The once subtle murmur of conversation turned into a roar, and the music adjusted to compensate.

It was probably a little after 10 PM when we decided to wrap things up. David said he had enough ideas to kick around and that we would touch base tomorrow. We shook hands, and David left the bar, heading back to his room. I had a hunch he would stay up all night long writing and organizing his thoughts. Who knows, maybe he wasn't joking about the cocaine?

I texted Mia's friend, Margot. [My name is Deputy Tyson

Wild. I'm looking into Mia Sophia's death. I was hoping I could ask you a few questions.]

I wasn't sure if I'd get a reply.

It wasn't late by LA standards. But a text from a cop in the middle of the night might not be Margot's highest priority to return.

I hung out in the booth for a moment, taking in the scenery. The bar was filled with pretty people, impeccably dressed. There were tight dresses and low-cut tops. Men in casual business attire. There were expensive watches and glittering diamonds dangling from necklaces, accenting svelte collarbones.

I recognized a few celebrities.

The hotel bar was the kind of place where the famous could drift about almost unseen. It was one of the reasons they came here. A private playground in the middle of the Los Angeles jungle. There were no paparazzi inside. No one to chronicle your ill-advised indulgences. At least, not until you left the hotel property. Outside, there was a gaggle of paparazzi waiting to spring out of the bushes to capture embarrassing moments. Inside, the hotel was a sanctuary for the elite.

A text from Margot dinged my phone. *[Why do you want to talk to me?]*

[You two were friends at one point, weren't you?]

[Yeah, but not anymore. I hadn't seen Mia in a long time before her death. I don't know how talking to me is going to help your investigation.]

[Just trying to get a sense of who she was.]

[Read the gossip blogs.]

[That's not the information I'm looking for.]

[She got carried away with the drugs, drank too much, and drowned. What is there to investigate?]

[I was the one who pulled her out of the pool. Call it a personal interest. I think she may have been murdered.]

My mildly inebriated eyes stared at the screen, waiting for a reply. Several minutes passed without one. Then I saw a text bubble forming on the screen. An instant later, another message buzzed through from Margot.

[I'm working. Can we talk about this later?]

[Sure. Where do you work?]

[Girls Unlimited.]

[I could stop by...]

[Rent is due. I don't have time for chitchat.]

[I'll be a paying customer.]

The screen was blank for a moment.

[Ask for Jade. That's my stage name.]

I slipped the phone into my pocket and slid out of the booth. It looked like I'd be paying a visit to the infamous strip club, strictly for professional reasons, of course.

I left the hotel bar and stepped onto the sidewalk. Engines rumbled as cars barreled down Sunset Boulevard. Brilliant headlights squinted my eyes after an evening in the dim bar.

The smell of exhaust filled the air. Buildings were illuminated with strategically placed lighting, and the glow of neon spilled across the boulevard. Billboards advertising movies and television shows towered overhead. Iconic structures lined the street.

Girls Unlimited was only a few blocks away. Everything was at your fingertips in West Hollywood.

I strolled down the sidewalk, and the cool California air blew through my hair. Pink and blue neon lights flickered. The light tubes were curved into the outline of exotic dancers. Several outlines, attached to the side of the building, flickered through different poses, giving the illusion of movement. Overhead, *GIRLS UNLIMITED* shone bright and buzzed. Moths and gnats swirled around the glowing tubes.

I stepped underneath a black awning and flashed my badge to the bouncer, who wore a dark gray suit with a black shirt. He waved me inside, then tapped his earbud and communicated with somebody inside the club. I couldn't hear exactly what he said. Then he shouted to the cashier. "No cover."

I nodded and smiled at the cashier, then strutted inside.

Music pumped through speakers, and spotlights slashed the foggy air. Girls in spike-heeled shoes hugged chrome poles, twirling around, performing acrobatic feats worthy of an Olympic competition. They pranced like show ponies atop mirrored stages, undulating in rhythm to the beat. Dollar bills hung from G-strings. Voluptuous curves were on full display. Skin shimmered with moisturizer. Perky melons jiggled and bounced.

The place smelled like cheap perfume, watered-down

whiskey, and bad decisions. Guys drooled on themselves, huddled around the stages. Girls writhed, rubbing their wares against lustful laps. I was pretty sure in the dark corners there was a little more than just lap dances going on.

A short man wearing a maroon leather blazer approached. He had dark hair, thinning on top, and a big nose. I noticed he had an earbud. The door guy had no doubt alerted him to my presence. I'm sure word was spreading through the club that law enforcement had arrived, allowing the girls to desist from any illicit activity.

The short man greeted me with a smile. "How can I help you this evening?"

"I'm looking for Jade."

"She in any trouble?"

"No. Nothing like that. Personal business. Relax, I'm just here to have fun."

The manager seemed relieved. "Excellent." His beady eyes scanned the club. "She's right over there," he said, pointing to the gorgeous brunette giving a gentleman what looked like a mighty fine lap dance. "Why don't you have a seat, make yourself comfortable. First round's on the house. I'll send Jade over as soon as she's done with her client."

I nodded appreciatively and found a seat not far from the stage and surveyed the talent. This place was full of it. There was something for everyone here. No matter what your taste, you could find the woman of your dreams—willing to be yours until the money ran out. Blondes, brunettes, redheads. Tall girls, skinny girls, healthy girls. There were retro-pinup Queens. Goth girls with raven black hair and black fingernails. Punk rock girls with blonde hair, blue hair, pixie cuts, and pigtails.

The bass drum thumped my chest, and the DJ introduced performers to the stage. "Charity, stage II. Charity, stage II!"

I watched the manager meander over to Jade and whisper in her ear. Her eyes flicked to me for a moment, then darted away.

A waitress in black lingerie, garter belt, and fishnet stockings pranced by my table. She had short dark hair, cut in a severe, stylish bob. "What can I get you?"

"Whisky. Rocks."

She nodded, spun around, and strutted to the bar. It was hard not to follow her with my eyes for a moment.

I thought about JD and wondered how things were going back in Coconut Key. I figured he'd love this place. But Sloan seemed to have tamed his wandering eye for the moment.

The waitress returned with my glass and set it on the table before me. I took a sip, and it was anything but smooth. But by this point in the evening, I had already downed several and wasn't as picky.

Jade sat with her client for another few minutes, then climbed out of his lap and got dressed—and when I say dressed, I mean she put on her bra. She bent over and gave her client a kiss on the cheek, then spun around and sauntered in my direction.

8

It was easy to see how Margot had picked her stage name, *Jade*. Her emerald eyes were almost luminescent. They caught the subtlest amount of light and reflected it, almost like a cat's eyes. Her dark hair accentuated her creamy skin that was lightly speckled with freckles across the nose and cheeks. Her red, full lips could spark lustful fantasies.

Her feline form pranced toward me as if she were stalking her prey. Her gaze never left mine. Though I had to admit, my eyes may have observed the black-lace bra that contained her buoyant orbs.

"You're Tyson?"

"In the flesh."

She plopped into my lap and flung her arm around me. "I'm on the clock. It's $20 a dance. Cash. What do you want to know?"

She was all business.

We were midway through the song—she would start peeling out of the frilly garments at the beginning of the next tune. The DJ certainly wasn't playing the extended radio edits. These were the short cuts. All the songs were about 2 minutes long, if that. The idea was to squeeze as many dances out of the clients as possible.

"Tracy told me that Mia stayed with you when she first moved to Los Angeles," I said.

"I told her she could crash on my couch. She stayed with me for a few months while she was looking for a job. But when she got big and famous, she sure didn't return the favor."

"You needed help?"

"Let's just say my career didn't take off like hers did. I had asked her to put in a good word for me with her agent." Jade frowned and shook her head. "But she never lifted a finger to help me. I was part of her old life, and she wanted nothing to do with her old life. It surprised me a little."

The song ended, and Jade climbed out of my lap. She reached her delicate hands behind her back and unclasped her bra. The straps fell from her shoulders, and she shimmied out of the garment and tossed it on the chair beside me. Her glorious endowments bounced free.

I couldn't help but focus on them. I swallowed hard, losing my concentration.

Jade was used to it. This wasn't the kind of place where you had to maintain eye contact. The whole point was to indulge in your carnal desires.

She began to move in hypnotic ways.

I refocused my mind. "Why did it surprise you?"

"Because... I had dirt on her."

"What kind of dirt?"

"I would never use it. I'm not that kind of person. Maybe that's why she ignored me. She knew her secrets would be safe with me."

Jade spun around and gave me a look at her backside. Taut and firm. She bent over and wiggled her hips.

She had a nice wiggle.

I took a deep breath. My heart beat a little faster. Suddenly it felt stuffy inside the club.

Concentrate.

"What secret?"

Jade spun around and straddled me. She slid up my body and pushed her bosoms into my face.

She was good at her job. One dance wasn't enough. I had no doubt she had plenty of repeat customers.

Jade grabbed my hands and put them on the outside of her thighs. I traced her smooth skin up to her hips. She was giving me a little taste of the merchandise. The sultry vixen spun around and placed her cheeks in my lap and did her best to polish the surface of my slacks. She leaned back against my chest, and her red lips tickled my ear as she whispered, "Nikki Griffin."

"Who's Nikki Griffin?" I asked.

Jade pulled away and her face scrunched up, looking at me

like I was crazy. "Mia's secret. For a cop, you don't know much."

"I'm not from around here."

"Ah," she said. Then confusion twisted her face. "If you're not from around here, why are you looking into her case?"

"A favor to her mother."

Jade climbed out of my lap, stood up, and undulated. She jiggled her wares, then dropped to her knees and placed her face in my lap, teasing me. Then she slid up my body again.

"There was no love lost between Mia and her mother. Now she's trying to play the poor pathetic victim? Please. Tracy was shitty to Mia."

"I guess she's trying to make amends."

"Little late for that, don't you think?"

"Who's Nikki Griffin?"

9

The song ended way too soon, and Jade stopped dancing. I dug into my pocket, peeled off a $20 from my money clip, and handed it to her. She stuffed it into her shoe, put on her bra, then sat in the chair next to me.

Girls typically danced every other song. We had a song to chat, then she'd be gone if I didn't fork over another $20. I had a fat stack and intended to stay as long as I needed to. I might even be tempted to stay longer.

"Nikki was a way for Mia to get off my couch and into her own apartment," Jade said.

"How so?"

"Nikki is very good about finding the young and beautiful. If you hadn't noticed, this town is all about *young and beautiful*. The trouble is, being young and beautiful often comes along with being broke. That's where Nikki comes in. Nikki has the connections."

"Is she an agent?"

Jade seemed amused by the phrase. "Of sorts."

"I think I'm beginning to figure out what you mean."

"Nikki facilitates arrangements between young girls and the wealthy and powerful. If you know what I mean."

"She's a madam."

"A very respectable, high-class madam. Discreet. And that's part of the allure. Nikki has a reputation. The girls know that if they work for her, they'll be paid well, treated right, and no one will find out about their dirty little secret."

"You introduced her to Nikki. I take it you worked for Nikki?"

"I did what I had to do. I'm not proud of it." She glanced around the club. "I don't really like working here, but it beats sleeping with perverted old men."

"How long ago did Mia work for Nikki?"

"A few years ago. Ancient history in this town."

"How long did Mia do that kind of work?"

"Not long. A few months. I don't think she was cut out for it. Not many girls are."

"Did that mess with her head?"

"I think that kind of thing messes with every girl's head that does it."

"When did Mia get into drugs?"

Jade chuckled. "Everyone in Hollywood is into drugs. It's

everywhere. Plus, when you've got to bang some guy you're not really into, it helps to be a little loaded. Some people can handle their high, some people can't."

"Mia would have met a lot of influential people working for Nikki, right? People that could help her career."

"I'm sure she did."

"Mia got ahead somehow," I said.

Jade shrugged. "Sometimes you gotta give a little head to get ahead. Look, I don't really know who she met during that time. She didn't talk about it much, and that was about the time we stopped being friends. I think part of her resented me for getting her into it. But hey, she was an adult, she could make her own decisions. When she got out of it, I don't think she liked being reminded that she ever did it."

The song ended.

"Another dance?" Jade asked.

"Absolutely."

Jade peeled off her bra again and began her routine. She changed it up a little this time. It was more sensual, if that was even possible. The first time was pretty stimulating. I figured the more you spent, the better the dances got.

"You know how I can get in touch with Nikki?"

"I'll give you her number. But you didn't get it from me. I don't want to get involved in this."

"Who are you afraid of?"

She slid up my body. "If what you say is true, and Mia was murdered, somebody had to have a pretty good reason."

"Like you said, maybe it was just a drug overdose," I said, playing devil's advocate.

"I think you underestimate how powerful some people are in this town. How nervous they are right now."

"Nervous?"

"Haven't you been keeping up with current events? A lot of people have abused their power over the years. It's coming back to bite them in the ass."

"You think Mia was going to make allegations against someone powerful?"

Jade shrugged. "I don't know. Maybe."

"Seems like an odd time to do that just as she was achieving notoriety."

"Maybe she figured her newfound stardom gave her the leverage to speak out? I guess we'll never know."

10

The waitress brought another round, and I stayed for a few more dances, trying to squeeze as much information out of Jade as possible. She was happy to squeeze as much money out of my wallet as she could.

Seemed like a win-win scenario.

I settled the tab and thanked Margot/Jade for her time. She told me to come back any time.

I could tell she had a lot of mixed emotions about Mia. It was a subject she had kept to herself for a long time. Talking about it seemed to be cathartic for her. Jade got to spill the beans on Mia's dirty little secret. At the same time, maybe she was helping me get one step closer to the truth.

Jade moved on to another client, and the manager's eyes followed me as I strolled toward the exit. We gave each other a subtle nod, and there was an uncomfortable smile on his face.

I think he was happy I was leaving.

No doubt a place like this had run-ins with the law on a regular basis. I knew from experience, you couldn't keep a place like this operating without greasing a few palms. A shady cop could make life hell for the management. Persistent raids looking for violations, visits from the Fire Marshal, the City Health Inspector, Alcoholic Beverage Control—anybody in the food chain that had an interest in making sure the operation was up to code. All of those people could appear with their hand out.

I nodded to the bouncer as I stepped onto the sidewalk. Cars buzzed up and down the boulevard. It was near 2 AM, but the city didn't seem like it had any intention of slowing down. The Hollywood Hills loomed above the strip, houses perched on hillsides with stilts and pylons. The hills had secrets of their own.

I ambled down the sidewalk, making my way back to the hotel, passing drunk revelers. At the next block, I crossed the street, slipped into the secluded entrance of the Château, and made my way up to my suite.

I sent a text to Isabella, my former handler at *Cobra Company,* and asked for information on Nikki Griffin. I set the phone on the nightstand by the bed, peeled out of my suit, brushed my teeth, and climbed into bed.

I had a restless sleep, tossing and turning all night, having weird dreams about the night Mia Sophia died.

The morning sun slipped through a narrow gap in the blinds, painting a brilliant line across the floor and part of the bed.

I yawned and stretched and wiped the sleep from my eyes. When I reached for my phone, I saw there was a reply from Isabella. I swiped the screen and surveyed her texts. She sent me a full dossier on Nikki Griffin. The infamous Hollywood madam had two residences. One in the hills, and one in Malibu. The dossier included several pictures and background information. There was also a snarky note from Isabella. [What's the matter? Are you lonely? Looking for entertainment?]

It made me chuckle.

I pulled myself out of bed, showered, got dressed, then headed down to the lobby for breakfast. David didn't mention what time we would reconnect today, so I shot him a quick text and asked if he'd like to join me. He responded a moment later and said he'd be down shortly.

The host seated me at a table, and David arrived a few minutes afterward. An excited grin curled his face. "I think I've got this whole thing pretty much mapped out—in broad strokes, anyway."

"That was quick."

"It's amazing what you can accomplish with an endless supply of coffee."

He looked like he hadn't slept much. "I'll show you what I've got after breakfast."

Scrambled eggs, hash browns, bacon, toast, and orange juice started the day off right. The dining area was filled with the subtle murmur of conversation and the clinking of silverware against plates. The smell of fresh coffee permeated the air. It was calm and relaxed. The chaos of the night had evaporated with the morning sun.

After we ate, we went to David's suite, and he showed me his outline. Each episode was labeled with the major complications and the twist. We talked briefly about the proposed episodes, and I filled him in on additional details and gave him guidance on authenticity. We spent the morning working out the finer details but still keeping it broad.

"We're creating a roadmap for the writers to follow. They'll fill in the blanks, we just need to keep them from going off course," David said. Then he added with derision, "You know writers..."

We ordered room service for lunch, and by the afternoon, we had pretty much come up with an overview and bullet points for each episode. I could see the whole thing coming together.

"I've been keeping detailed daily journals, if that's helpful," I said.

David's eyes widened. "Why didn't you say something sooner?"

I shrugged. "I don't know. They're personal. Probably pretty boring. I just write about my day, so I don't forget about what happened in my life. When I'm old and senile, if I make it that far, I can look back."

"I'd love to see them."

I considered it.

I kept hearing David say the phrase, "We're in the second *Golden Age* of television."

TV used to be a place where movie stars went after their film careers had run their course. It was seen as a downgrade. Now, with long-form episodic television, and streaming networks creating binge-able content, television had opened up new possibilities. No longer was it looked down upon. With 12 or 24 episodes per season, there was an ability to tell stories that were more complex and more involved than any movie could be.

The process is what let me keep *Diver Down*, and for that, I was grateful.

David said he would spend the rest of the afternoon and evening going over everything we had worked on, revising it, adding to it, and possibly rearranging things. He said we'd touch base to evaluate the revisions before putting it into a presentable *treatment* to give to the studio. It was often referred to as a *Series Bible*—the immutable rules the show would follow.

With the afternoon to myself, I decided it was time to meet Nikki Griffin.

11

"Nikki, my name is Tyson Wild. I'm hoping you can help me," I said into the phone when I was back in my suite.

"I'd love to help you, darling. How did you get my number?"

"A former employee."

"Who?" she asked, cautiously intrigued.

"The lady wishes to remain anonymous," I said.

"I'm very discreet. You can tell me."

"I never break my word."

"I only work with referrals from people I know well. Seems we might be at an impasse."

"I was hoping you could tell me about Mia Sophia."

The line was silent for a moment.

"I don't gossip about the dead. If you're working for one of those sleazy tabloids—"

"I'm not working for the tabloids. I'm investigating her death."

"You're a cop?"

"Not local. Deputy Sheriff in Florida."

"A little bit out of your jurisdiction, aren't you, Deputy?"

"I'm working in an unofficial capacity."

"I'm afraid I don't know any more than what I read on the Internet."

"Can you think of anyone who may have wanted to harm her?"

There was another long pause.

"As I mentioned, Deputy. I'm very discreet. I don't discuss clients or employees."

"So, Mia was an employee?"

"Goodbye, Deputy Wild."

She ended the call.

Her unwillingness to talk on the phone didn't surprise me. I would have to try other tactics.

I called Lyric Stone, the reporter that had acquired Mia's autopsy report. Her phone went straight to voicemail, and I left a message. Reporters were always eager to break a story, and I figured I had a good chance of getting a call back.

It only took a few minutes.

After we made introductions, Lyric asked, "Your message

mentioned you were looking into Mia Sophia's death. How can I help you?"

"I thought you might have turned up some interesting leads?"

"Not really. Nobody will talk to me. The LAPD has closed the case. There is nothing to discuss, they say."

"Tell me what you really think."

"I think something's funny. But that's my nature."

"Care to elaborate?"

"About my nature, or about what I think is odd?"

"I'm staying at the Château. Perhaps we can discuss this over drinks?"

"Are you looking for a date, Deputy Wild, or information?"

"I don't need a date. And certainly not with a reporter."

"What do you have against reporters?"

"Let's just say I've been burned a few times."

There was another pause.

"How do I know you're who you say you are?"

"Call Sheriff Daniels at the Coconut County Sheriff's Department."

"I'm not too keen on meeting strangers right now."

"One can never be too careful these days," I cautioned.

"Let's just say I have reason to be concerned." She paused. After a moment, curiosity got the best of her. "I'm gonna make some phone calls. If you check out, how does 8 PM sound?"

"Perfect."

"Send me a pic, so I know who to look for."

After I hung up, I took a selfie and texted it to her.

JD called a few minutes later. "Oh, my God!"

"What is it now?"

"That girl is just amazing." He could only be talking about Sloan.

"So you've said. Numerous times."

"She's just fun to be with."

"That's good. I'm glad you're enjoying yourself."

"I dropped her off at the airport, and I got another kiss on the cheek."

"That's a little tame for your standards."

"I don't mind taking this one slow."

"When are you coming out?" I asked.

"Not sure. I've got some stuff to do around here. I'll probably fly out in the morning."

"Give me your flight details when you have them, and I'll have the driver pick you up."

"You getting into anything interesting out there?" JD asked.

"I found a place you'd love. At least, the *old you* would love. I'm not so sure about the *new you*. It might be too exciting."

"What do you mean the *old me*? I haven't changed."

I chuckled. "Are you even allowed to go to strip clubs anymore?"

JD scoffed. "It's not like I'm in a relationship. I'm in pursuit. I have no restraints."

"Not yet."

"Please, you know I cannot be caged. I'm a wild animal that needs to roam free," he said dramatically.

I rolled my eyes and told him I'd talk to him later.

I put on a pair of shorts and a T-shirt and went for a jog around West Hollywood. I got quite a few honks and catcalls—not from whom I was looking to get catcalls from, but a compliment is a compliment, I guess.

The hills made it considerably more challenging than the flats of Coconut Key. By the time I returned to the hotel, my body was drenched with sweat.

I took a shower, changed into a *Di Fiore* suit, then headed down to the dining room for dinner. It was a modern take on classic American cuisine. I ordered the New York Steak Frites and a glass of wine—a grilled New York strip with an herb-butter shallot bordelaise sauce and french fries. The steak was tender and juicy, and the fries were crisp. It was hard to go wrong with a dish like that.

There was a subtle note at the bottom of the menu that reminded patrons not to take photos within the restaurant. It was usually lined with celebrities. There was an Oscar-winning actress at the table next to me having a discreet dinner with a gentleman I didn't recognize. That was par for the course around here.

After dinner, I ambled to the bar and leaned against the counter. I gave a nod, and the bartender moved to me. "What can I get for you?"

"Are you Marcel?"

He nodded.

He had curly dark hair, a thin mustache, and a trimmed goatee.

"You were working the night Mia Sophia died," I said.

"Yeah, but if you're with the press, I'm not talking."

I flashed my shiny gold badge. "I'm investigating the case."

"Look, I told the cops everything I know."

"Just a few follow-up questions."

His face tensed with discomfort. "Look, I only served her two drinks. I don't know what she had before she got here or after she left. If you want to know anything else, you can talk to my lawyer."

He started to turn away.

"Off the record. I'm not trying to get you in trouble or held liable for what happened."

Marcel hesitated.

"Who was she with that night?"

Marcel eyed me for a long moment.

"While you're thinking about what to say, you can pour me a glass of whiskey."

Marcel grabbed a bottle from the well.

"No. The *James Burke Reserve.*" I told him to put it on my tab.

Marcel grabbed the bottle of top-shelf liquor, spun it around, and poured a glass. He slid the smooth amber whiskey across the counter, and I gave a nod of appreciation.

"She came in by herself. Ordered a drink from me, and she sat at that booth back there," he said, pointing. "She waited there for a few minutes, then she met with Desmond Ross."

I lifted a curious eyebrow. "Who's Desmond Ross?"

Marcel was stunned at my ignorance. His eyes widened with disbelief.

12

"**D**esmond Ross is one of the biggest producers in Hollywood," Marcel said.

"Does he come in here a lot?" I asked.

Marcel shrugged. "I guess so."

"What was the context of their conversation?"

His face crinkled. "Do you think I can hear what they were talking about from here?"

"Body language speaks louder than words. Were they getting along? Were they having a fight? Was it tense, or casual?"

Marcel thought about it for a moment. "I guess it looked a little strained. Honestly, it was a busy night. I wasn't really paying attention."

"Did Mia look to be coherent that night?"

His eyes narrowed at me. "I wouldn't have served her if she wasn't." He hesitated, then admitted, "I thought she might have been a little coked up. But that's not unusual around here."

"Did you see her leave the bar?"

"I didn't. It was pretty crowded that night."

"I remember. I was here."

He looked at me, surveying my facial features. "That's right. You do look familiar. You were here with Chloe-C and that guy from that '80s band... What's his name?"

He'd mistaken JD. I went along with it. "Yeah. You've got a good memory."

A glimmer of recognition flickered in his eyes. He had a better memory than he was letting on.

"I'm staying in the hotel. If you can think of anything else that might be helpful, let me know."

"Sure thing," he said.

A sultry redhead with emerald eyes and porcelain skin pulled up to the bar next to me.

I was a sucker for redheads.

"You must be Tyson Wild," she said.

"You must be Lyric Stone."

We shook hands.

"Pleasure to make your acquaintance," I said.

"Likewise, Deputy Wild."

I nodded to the empty booth in the corner where Mia
Sophia had once met with Desmond Ross.

Lyric ordered a whiskey, rocks from Marcel before we left
the bar.

A woman after my own heart.

We slid into the comfy seats of the curved booth. The
bordeaux red lighting made the bar seem illicit and sinful.

"I assume I passed your background check?" I said.

"I checked with your Sheriff Daniels."

"And?"

"He had *relatively* good things to say. But he did give me a
warning."

I lifted my brow. "Oh, really?"

"He told me not to let you break my heart."

I chuckled. "And how did you respond?"

"I told him I don't have a heart to break."

I chuckled again, lifted my glass, and we toasted.

"So, you think Mia was murdered?" she asked.

"I'm not ruling out the possibility. What can you tell me?"

Lyric shrugged. "I can tell you she was dating Zach Ward.
But they broke up recently."

"Who's Zach Ward?"

"You certainly aren't a pop-culture aficionado, are you?"

"It's not on my priority list."

"He's the lead on that hit TV show *The Unstoppables*."

"Never heard of it."

She chuckled. "You are not from around here."

"I'll take that as a compliment."

"You should. This town lives, sleeps, eats, and breathes the business. Actually, it's kind of refreshing to speak with someone who isn't involved."

"I hate to disappoint, but I am involved."

She lifted a curious brow. "Oh, really? How so?"

"Now I'm beginning to wonder about your pop-culture acumen. The Bree Taylor project..."

A wave of recognition flashed in her eyes. "You're *that* Tyson Wild."

"I am. Guilty as charged."

"So, you do multimillion-dollar Hollywood deals and moonlight as a deputy sheriff in a small beach town?"

"Volunteer."

"Giving back to the community. I can respect that."

"Call it an obsession."

"Truth, justice, and the American way?"

"Something like that."

"Let me guess... Former military?" Her eyes narrowed, sizing me up. "Maybe I'm reaching, but I'm going to say Navy SEALs."

"Among other things. Either you've done your homework, or you have a hell of an intuition. And I don't think you have the security clearance to do the homework."

"Sounds serious, and intriguing." There was a delightful sparkle in her eyes.

Her eyes weren't bad to look at. Not bad at all.

"So tell me about Zach Ward, and why they broke up?"

"Who really knows what happens between two people? But I'm sure the paparazzi photos of Zach with Tricia Marlowe didn't help their relationship."

"Who is Tricia Marlowe?"

"Another up-and-comer. You might recognize her from *The Zone*."

"I rarely watch TV." I paused. "What do you know about Mia's relationship with Desmond Ross?"

Her eyes filled with potential stories to tell. "Desmond launched her career. She wouldn't have gotten the new series without him. He was executive producer." Lyric leaned in and whispered. "Now, I don't have any confirmation on this, but... word is that she met Desmond through..." she chose her words, "less than reputable means."

"Nikki Griffin."

Lyric looked impressed. "I see you do your homework as well."

"I don't suck at my job."

She measured my response. "I like a confident man."

I smiled. "Good to know."

"I thought you weren't looking for a date."

"I'm not."

"Good. Because you are *so* not my type."

I grinned. I knew that game. "And what is your type?"

She hesitated coyly. "Not you."

I smiled again, seeing through her protest. "I spoke with Nikki Griffin, but she wasn't very forthcoming."

"Not surprising." Lyric paused. "Look, it's all rumor and speculation. I've never been able to get concrete proof. And you know how this town is... People start rumors to sabotage a competitor's career. Who knows if there's any truth to it. The goal is to place doubt in the mind. And sometimes that doubt can linger for an eternity. Just ask Greg Richards."

There were awful rumors swirling around about the famous actor and had been for years.

"Nikki didn't confirm that Mia had ever worked for her," I said. "But she didn't deny it either. And she wasn't keen to talk about it."

"Nikki's got enough dirt to bring just about everyone in Hollywood down. I can only imagine the headlines if Nikki ever went public with the names in her little black book. Maybe that's her insurance policy?"

"You mentioned on the phone that you were getting a little pushback," I said.

"That's one way to put it." Lyric took a deep breath. "My house was broken into, my laptop was stolen. My tires were slashed. A note was left on my desk to quit being so nosy."

"I'd say that's pushback."

"I dropped the story. I'm all about breaking news, but I'm not too keen on ending up face down in a pool, or cut up in an alley." She let out a deep exhale. "I gotta hand it to you, you've got balls. This investigation of yours might end up pissing a few people off. People you probably don't want pissed off."

I smirked. "I'm used to upsetting people. I like to think of it as a special skill."

"Everybody's got a gift, don't they?"

I grinned again. "Indeed."

I lifted my glass, and we toasted. I watched her wrap her plump lips around the glass and finish the whiskey.

"Where can I find Zach Ward and Desmond Ross?"

She rattled off a list of bars that they frequented, and she promised to text me Desmond's office address.

Her parting words were, "Be careful, Deputy Wild. You seem like a decent guy. Those are already in short supply."

13

I had some time to kill. The clubs on Sunset wouldn't get happening until 11 PM. I figured I would swing by *Skyline, Opal, Prism*, and the *Crescent Club*—all places Lyric said that Zach Ward frequented.

Since Jack was coming into town tomorrow, I figured it might be a good idea to stock up on liquor. The minibar prices were exorbitant, and it didn't make sense when there was a liquor store just down the street. Even though the studio was picking up the tab, it seemed wasteful.

I left the hotel and walked down Sunset. Cars buzzed up and down the boulevard. The night brimmed with possibilities, and the denizens of Hollywood would descend from the hills and soon be hitting the clubs.

The door chime rang as I pushed into the liquor store. I nodded at the older man behind the counter. He was thin with gray hair, saggy eyes, and rosy cheeks. He looked like he hit the bottle pretty hard after closing time. Maybe even before. I'm sure he put the employee discount to good use.

There was nobody else in the store.

The shelves were lined with rows of whiskey, rum, vodka, and tequila. The center aisles were filled with wine racks, mostly from California vineyards.

I perused the selection of fine whiskey and aged rum. Two bottles would do the trick. I didn't want to carry back a heavy case of whiskey.

The door chimed again as two men entered.

I casually glanced at the door, and I didn't like what I saw.

I didn't like it at all.

They weren't really men—two boys, judging by their size and frame. Black ski masks concealed their faces, and it didn't take a rocket scientist to figure out what they wanted.

In a flash, the clerk found himself on the business end of a shiny silver semi-automatic pistol.

"Give me the fucking money!"

The clerk raised his hands in the air, cautiously, then slowly moved to the register.

The two thugs may have put effort into concealing their identities, but the dipshits wore brightly colored shirts that were easily identifiable. The thug with the silver pistol wore a yellow basketball jersey with the number 8 on it. His comrade wore a purple jersey with the number 21.

Purple swung his pistol toward me. The barrel trembled slightly. "Don't fucking move! Be cool, and nobody gets hurt."

I set the bottle of whiskey on the shelf and raised my hands in surrender.

"Hurry up, motherfucker!" Yellow commanded, his weapon turned sideways, aimed at the clerk in poor tactical form.

The clerk opened the money drawer and snatched the cash. He pulled out fat stacks and set them on the counter. $20s, $10s, $5s, and a lot of $1s. The total haul was $600 or $700. Fear swelled the clerk's eyes, and rage boiled under his skin.

Yellow grabbed the cash and said, "Have a nice day, motherfucker!"

He darted for the door.

Purple backed away from me, spun around, and followed.

BANG!

A deafening blast rattled the liquor store. Smoke wafted from the barrel of a 9mm. The clerk had grabbed a gun from underneath the counter and squeezed the trigger.

Purple smacked the tile floor and groaned in agony, crimson blood staining his jersey.

The door chimed as Yellow sprinted out. His sneakers smacked against the sidewalk as he took off running.

Purple writhed and wailed.

I dashed across the liquor store to the boy and kicked his pistol out of reach. I dropped to my knees and applied pressure to the wound. I shouted to the clerk, "Call 911!"

He stood there for a moment, stunned, still aiming the pistol at the downed thief.

"Call 911!"

He hesitated for another moment, then dialed emergency services.

Red blood seeped through my fingers as I tried to stem the incessant tide spewing from the boy's thoracic cavity. The warm liquid pulsed with the beat of his heart. Every second grew more precarious. "Hang in there, kid."

The kid's eyes filled with panic behind the ski mask. He and his buddy had probably been doing this kind of thing for a while without so much as a scratch.

Today his luck ran out.

"That's the third time in four months those little pricks have hit the store," the clerk growled.

I had no doubt that he was more than willing to put more bullets into the kid. I could understand his level of frustration.

"How does it feel, ya little shit?" the clerk shouted at the thug. "You ought to think twice about pulling a gun on somebody. Not too fun being on the other end of it, is it?"

14

I did my best until the EMTs arrived. They took over and stabilized the kid, then loaded him into the back of the ambulance.

When they pulled his mask off, I could see that the kid was 14, maybe 15 at most.

I stood on the sidewalk, watching as the EMTs closed the rear doors. They scurried around to the passenger compartment, then sped away with the siren blazing.

The police hadn't arrived yet.

My eyes caught sight of the yellow jersey across the street. Number 8 stood on the corner, watching. He wasn't wearing a ski mask any longer, but there was no mistaking him. My eyes locked with his, and he took off running.

Horns honked as I darted into the street, crossing Sunset, chasing after him. I must have looked like a maniac, my suit crusted with crimson blood.

I ran down a side street, and I saw Yellow veer into an alleyway.

When I rounded the corner, he was at the far end of the passage, near the dumpster. He dashed left on the sidewalk and disappeared down the next block.

I gave up and headed back to the liquor store. The kid was fast, and I was wearing dress shoes.

Red and blue lights flickered across the storefront as I returned. A patrol car had arrived, and officers were interviewing the clerk. Curious looks twisted their faces as I stepped to the storefront.

"Who the hell are you?" an officer asked.

I identified myself as a police officer and explained the situation and my involvement. I gave a brief statement, and they requested the security footage from the clerk.

The officers looked bored.

This was routine.

I was sure they had no intention of doing anything about it. I gave Officer Weaver a description of the kid that I chased into the alley. He noted it, took my information, and that was the end of it.

The officers climbed back into their patrol car, killed the lights, and pulled away from the curb.

"You should have let me kill that son-of-a-bitch," the clerk muttered.

"I'm sure you'll have another opportunity," I said dryly.

I pushed into the store and made my way down the aisle. I

grabbed two bottles of whiskey and brought them to the counter. The clerk rang me up, and I was on my way.

You'd think that walking down the Sunset Strip in a bloody suit, holding two brown bags of liquor, would cause an inordinate amount of stares. But nobody paid any attention to me at all.

Go figure.

I took off my jacket, folded it over, and tried to cover the blood stain on my shirt as I walked through the hotel lobby.

In my room, I pulled the whiskey bottles from their bags and set them on the counter, then peeled out of my bloody suit. I took a shower, changed into another suit, then called room service and sent my soiled garments out for cleaning.

I wasn't sure the stains would come out.

My phone buzzed with a call from Lyric. "You got a minute?"

"For you, I've got more than a minute."

"I did some digging."

"I thought you had dropped your investigation?"

"Well, old habits die hard. And you've sparked my curiosity." She paused. "So, take this with a grain of salt. I have a source that has a source..."

"Okay..."

"The toxicology report was sent out to an independent lab for testing. My source, who has a source within that lab, swears that a large amount of fentanyl was found in Mia's blood along with the heroin, cocaine, and alcohol."

"The fentanyl didn't make it into the final report," I said, my face twisted with confusion.

"I know."

"How much trust do you place in these *sources*?"

"A lot."

"Would you bet your life on it?"

She hesitated for a long moment. "Let me get back to you on that one. But I trust my source."

I thanked her for the info and told her to let me know if anything else came up.

It was almost II PM. I figured I'd hit *Opal* first. It was the closest bar to the hotel. The line of pretty people was around the corner, and I had no intention of waiting for hours to get in.

I cut the line and flashed my badge to the bouncer at the velvet rope. He unhooked the rope from the stanchion and waved me past. Another flash of my badge to the cashier, and I was inside the club.

Music thumped, and colored lights swirled. A sea of revelers undulated in rhythm to the beat.

The place was packed.

I surveyed the scene, looking for the VIP area. Movie stars didn't usually party with mere mortals. They sat at exclusive tables and drank from expensive bottles.

I pushed through the crowd, weaving my way to the far end of the club. There were lots of short skirts, high heels, and fake boobs.

Really, really nice fake boobs.

Beverly Hills surgeons had lots of practice.

There were gaudy purses and blinged-out cell phones and lots of shimmering earrings and necklaces.

I had looked up Zach Ward online and studied a few images of the leading actor. I kept a few for reference on my phone.

There was a section of the club that was roped off toward the back, and a bouncer stood guard. Pretty people lounged on couches and drank bottles of expensive champagne.

I surveyed the VIP area but didn't see who I was looking for. I approached the VIP bouncer and flashed my badge. "Looking for Zach Ward. Have you seen him?"

"He's not in tonight. He's usually here on Thursdays. Is he in some kind of trouble?"

The bouncer was looking for juicy gossip.

"No. I just need to ask him a few questions."

"This about Mia Sophia?"

I lifted a curious eyebrow. "It is, actually. Why do you ask?"

The bouncer shrugged. "They used to date. That's all. Plus, there was another cop in here asking about Zach a week ago."

"Well, we like to be thorough."

The bouncer surveyed me for a moment. "You might be able to catch him at *Skyline*. That's where the Panty Platoon hangs out."

"Panty Platoon?"

"Have you been living in the Stone Age, man?"

"I just thawed out. I've been frozen in a block of ice for the last 2,000 years."

He chuckled. "It's a group of young stars. They're always cruising the bars, picking up chicks. I mean, who could blame them. If I was rich, famous, and good-looking, I'd be hitting anything that walked." He paused. "I guess I'll just have to settle for *good looking*."

I grinned and we shook hands. "What's your name?"

"Tyrell."

"Good to meet you, Tyrell. My name is Tyson. Thanks for the info."

"Just remember I did you a solid."

"You're not planning on getting in trouble, are you?"

He grinned. "Nobody ever plans on getting in trouble. But it never hurts to have a friend *on the job.*" He paused. "You can't do anything about parking tickets, can you?"

The ivy-covered pavilion of *Skyline* offered a stunning view of the city. Lights of the LA basin twinkled like stars in the night. There were cozy white couches and chairs. Flowing sheer drapes rippled with the breeze. Candles flickered atop tables. Lounge chairs surrounded the outdoor pool, and the bar served up fresh cocktails. Music pumped through speakers, and pretty people mingled. It was an exclusive bar, and the clientele was carefully curated. If you were a celebrity, you bypassed the chaotic line and were ushered to an exclusive area.

I found Zach poolside. He was with a few members of the *platoon* and Tricia Marlowe.

Zach had piercing blue eyes, brown hair, and a square head that looked like it belonged on television. He almost looked cartoonish in person. A constant insincere smile was permanently etched on his face, revealing pearly white teeth that almost seemed to glow. He was a man that knew people were always looking at him.

Tricia Marlowe was a platinum blonde with shoulder-length hair coiffed to perfection. She reminded me of an old-school Hollywood starlet. She wore a black one-piece that hugged her pert form. The halter top had a low V-cut, revealing what looked to be all-natural endowments. A rarity in this town.

I flashed my badge as I approached. I'm pretty sure everyone assumed I was LA County. "I'd like to talk to you about Mia Sophia."

Zach's perpetual grin faded. "I already talked to the LAPD. Mia drowned. What more is there to say?"

"The autopsy report says she had alcohol, cocaine, and heroin in her system at the time of death."

"I guess she made some bad choices," Zach said.

I decided to roll with Lyric's information and see where it got me. "There was enough fentanyl in her system to kill a rhinoceros. If she didn't drown, she would have been dead anyway."

A wave of concern washed over Zach's face. "I guess she got a hold of some bad stuff."

"Any idea where she got it from?"

He shrugged. "I don't know. I don't do drugs."

Zach flashed that television smile again, but I could tell he was lying. I could see it in his eyes.

"Sure. No one in Hollywood does drugs," I said dryly. "Especially not the rich and famous."

"What are you getting at?"

"Maybe it was bad luck," I suggested. "Maybe she bought a bad batch from the wrong dealer. Who knows? Or maybe, somebody tainted her supply on purpose."

Zack's face twisted up. "Why would anyone do that?"

"You tell me."

He shrugged innocently.

"Did she have any enemies?"

"Everyone in Hollywood has enemies. But I can't imagine there was anyone who wanted to kill her. That's what you're suggesting, isn't it?"

"Why did you two break up?"

"Don't answer any more questions," Tricia advised.

Zach squirmed uncomfortably.

"If he doesn't have anything to hide, he's got nothing to worry about," I said to the blonde bombshell.

"I don't have anything to hide," Zach announced.

"Who had the most to gain by Mia's death?" I asked.

Without hesitation, Zach said, "June Foster."

"Who's that?"

"She was probably Mia's biggest competitor. The two hated each other. They were always up against each other at auditions, and June always lost out to Mia. June actually took over her role on the new show."

I glanced at Tricia. "What about you? Were you ever in competition with Mia?"

Tricia's eyes narrowed at me. "We're not the same type. And even if we were, Mia wouldn't have been competition for me."

"What you're suggesting sounds a little outrageous," Zach said. "I highly doubt June Foster paid Bhodi to lace Mia's drugs with fentanyl." The name slipped out, and I could tell Zach regretted it the minute it escaped from his lips.

"So, Bhodi was Mia's dealer?" I asked.

Zach grimaced. He looked around to make sure no one was listening. The rest of his *platoon* had drifted away the minute I flashed my badge. Zach leaned in and hissed, "Bhodi Hendrix. But you didn't hear that from me."

"Where can I find Bhodi?"

"He's at all the usual hotspots. Here, *Opal, Crescent Club, Prism.* He supplies all the celebrities with their party favors."

"How do I get in touch with him?"

Zach shifted uncomfortably again.

"I'll leave your name out of it," I assured.

"I can give you his number. But he won't call you back. Not from a number he doesn't recognize." Zach thought about it for a moment. A devious grin curled on his lips. "Tell him Blaine sent you."

"Who's Blaine?"

"A guy I don't like."

I entered Bhodi's number into my cell phone.

"What about Nikki Griffin?" I asked.

Zach rolled his eyes. "That's all bullshit."

"If you say so," Tricia added snidely.

Zach's eyes narrowed at her. "Please. Mia was not a hooker."

"She got to the top somehow, and it certainly wasn't on talent," Tricia quipped.

"Seriously? Have a little respect," Zach snapped.

Tricia's face crinkled. "Why are you defending her?"

"Because she's dead. She can't defend herself."

"I thought you were over her, but I guess not." Tricia sipped her drink.

"Why are you being like this?" Zach growled.

"Can we get back on topic?" I suggested, interrupting the quarrel. "What was Mia's relationship like with Desmond Ross?"

The two got quiet.

"I don't really know," Zach said.

"Did they ever sleep together?"

"We never talked about it, and I didn't ask."

Tricia bulged her tongue into her cheek and made a motion with her hand like she was sucking on something. It didn't take a rocket scientist to figure out what.

The gesture annoyed Zach. "She did not suck her way to the top."

"She didn't get there on talent, just saying," Tricia added. She'd had quite a few drinks, and her filter was nonexistent.

"You have to excuse her," Zach said. "She gets a little mouthy when she's drunk."

"You like it when I'm *mouthy*," she muttered. "Stop being a dick, or you're not going to get any mouthy-mouthy tonight."

Zach took a deep breath. "You ought to be looking into Rory Allen."

"Who's Rory Allen?" I asked.

16

"He's a nut job," Zach said. "Mia had to get a restraining order against him. He broke into her house one time. Threatened to kill her."

"What for?" I asked.

"I don't know. The voices in his head told him to do it?" he mocked.

"And you think Rory could have paid Bhodi to lace Mia's drugs with fentanyl because the voices told him to do it?" I asked with more than a trace of sarcasm.

Zach's face crinkled. "I don't know. I'm just making suggestions." He paused. "Are you sure it was the fentanyl that killed her?"

I shrugged. "Right now, I'm not sure of anything. Somebody could have pushed her into the pool, and she was too whacked out to do anything about it."

"Who would do something like that?"

"I've got a source that saw her with Desmond Ross that night."

Zach exchanged a glance with Tricia.

"You're not gonna catch me saying anything bad about Desmond," Zach said.

"Why not?"

"Because," he said, incredulous. "Going against that guy is career suicide."

"You're a big star," I said, smugly. "Surely, your career is safe."

Zach's eyes narrowed at me. "Desmond can blacklist anyone. Nobody's career is safe in Hollywood." He paused. "Look, I hope you get to the bottom of this. I really do. We didn't always see eye to eye, but Mia was a special girl."

Tricia's jealous eyes blazed into him.

It didn't go unnoticed.

Zach defended himself. "What!? Am I not allowed to care for someone I used to date? Someone who happens to be dead now? What the fuck is wrong with you?"

"What the fuck is wrong with *you*?" Tricia snapped back.

The platinum blonde spun around and stormed away.

"Excuse me. I have to do damage control."

Zach chased after Tricia.

I mingled through *Skyline*, taking in the sights. I had to admit, all the online reviews weren't wrong. This was one of the best views of all the nightclubs in West Hollywood.

I figured it was too late to pursue any more leads. I might as well have a little fun. I made my way through the good-looking crowd and ordered a whiskey at the bar.

A blonde shuffled next to me. She wore a black strapless dress that created a delightful valley of cleavage. She wasn't shy about showing it off either. "Excuse me, but I couldn't help notice you talking to Zach Ward. Are you two friends?"

"I guess you could call us acquaintances," I said.

"You think you could introduce me? I've had such a crush on him for, like, ever." She was like a giddy schoolgirl. "I mean, I just don't want to approach him randomly and come off like a total fan or a stalker." She chuckled, laughing it off.

"I thought you just said you were a fan?"

Her face soured. "I said I had a crush on him. And once he gets a taste of what's in these panties, he may just have a crush on me."

She had a few drinks and was a little on the sloppy side. She knew what she wanted, and she was determined to get it. The blonde was good looking, in a plastic sort of way, but it was the attitude that really killed it.

"If you're as desirable as you say you are, you don't need my help."

Her face scrunched up. "Dick!"

She spun around and stormed away.

I laughed. *Hollywood.*

My phone buzzed in my pocket, and I slid the device out and looked at the screen. It was a text from Lyric.

[*Find out anything interesting?*]

[Isn't it past your bedtime?]

[*I'm a big girl. I can stay up as late as I want.*]

[I just spoke with Zach Ward.]

[*And?*]

[Meet me at *Skyline*, and I'll tell you.]

[It's late, and I'm not waiting in that line. How about I meet you back at the hotel? I've got information you might find useful.]

[My room is #421]

[*Not your hotel room. The bar. Don't get ahead of yourself.*]

[When?]

[*20 minutes. I live close. In the hills.*]

[See you there.]

17

The hotel bar was crowded, but not overly so. The booths were full, but I managed to grab a table. I didn't see Lyric yet.

A waitress swung by, and I ordered a round for both of us. I gave her my room number, and she put it on my tab.

Lyric strutted into the bar a few minutes later. She had changed outfits and was wearing a skimpy blue dress that accented her red hair and creamy skin. It hugged all of her well-placed curves and took the eye on the delightful journey through captivating peaks and valleys. She had freshened up her makeup, which she didn't need, anyway.

I began to think her interest was more than just *business*.

I stood up as she arrived and offered her the seat across from me. "Thanks for coming."

"Well, I didn't have anything else to do," she said, feigning boredom.

I took a seat and lifted my glass. She clinked hers against

mine, then brought it to her beautiful lips. She stopped short of sipping it and examined the whiskey carefully. "I usually don't drink anything that I haven't seen poured myself." Her emerald eyes gazed into mine, searching for clues to my nature. "I don't think you're the type to roofie anyone."

"Are you sure about that?" I asked, taunting her.

"I guess we're about to find out." She took a sip of the liquor and swallowed it down. "In this town you learn to size up people pretty quickly. Everybody's full of shit. Except a rare few."

"What category do I fall into?"

She squinted, pretending to scrutinize me once again. "I'm gonna say the *rare few*."

"It's like an exclusive club," I said proudly.

"More like an endangered species."

I smiled. My eyes drank in her enticing form, her gorgeous face, her sultry eyes. "Nice dress. You look... not at all unattractive."

She arched a sassy eyebrow at me. "Is that your version of a compliment?"

"Yes, I do believe so."

"Don't get too excited. This is just drinks, and we're just discussing business."

"Do you always discuss business looking like this?"

"Like what?" she asked, acting oblivious.

I shrugged. "Oh, I don't know... stunning?"

She tried to hide a grin on her full lips. "Would you rather I had worn sweatpants and put my hair up in a bun?"

"Somehow, I think you could make any combination look good."

"Well, aren't you charming this evening?" She took another sip of her whiskey.

I feigned modesty. "I haven't unleashed my full charm yet."

She laughed. There was a trace of sarcasm in her voice when she said, "Please don't. I don't know if I could stand it, Captain Charm."

"I'll go easy on you. Since this is just business, let's get down to it."

"Tell me about your encounter with Zach Ward first."

I filled her in on the details. She soaked it all in. "I'm surprised he talked to you."

"Usually, I consider the ex-boyfriends suspects. But he didn't give me that impression. Tricia Marlowe seems like a real handful, though. But other than a general disdain for Mia, I don't think she had motive."

She played devil's advocate. "Maybe our imagination is running away with us? Maybe Mia died of an OD and an unfortunate circumstance. I mean, it's crazy to think that someone in the medical examiner's office altered the autopsy report, right?"

I shook my head. "I don't think we're the crazy ones."

Lyric took another sip, staining the glass with her lipstick.

"You know how when you think everyone else is crazy... then one day, you stop and wonder if maybe you're the one who's crazy?"

"You seem pretty sane to me."

"You just don't know me that well." There was a devious sparkle in her eyes.

"You said you had information."

"I tracked down a girl who worked for Nikki Griffin, supposedly at the same time as Mia."

"Did you speak with her?"

"Not yet. I'm gonna leave that up to you. I think you might get more out of her than me. Her real name is Devon Scott, but she goes by the stage name Amber Angel now."

"Stripper?"

Lyric shook her head. "Porn star. That ought to be right up your alley." She arched a sassy eyebrow and waited for my reaction.

"Does she still work for Nikki?"

"Not from what I hear."

"And who did you hear this from?"

"You know how it is with reporters and sources..." She had no intention of revealing any of them.

"You and your *sources*," I muttered.

"None of them have let me down yet," she assured.

"Where can I find Amber Angel?"

"You can give her agent a call in the morning. Who knows, maybe you can hire her? Do an *in-depth* investigation," she taunted.

"Where's the sport in paying for it?"

"So, you're all about the sport?"

"I like a challenge."

"Is that why there's no Mrs. Wild? Too busy looking for the next conquest?"

"What do you know about Rory Allen?" I said, changing the subject.

"Did I hit a sore spot?" she asked with a grin.

I continued to push in a different direction. "Rory Allen?"

Her eyes gleamed with confidence. "Definitely a sore spot."

"Not a sore spot. I'm just taking life as it comes. And please explain to me why an attractive, driven woman such as your-self is single?"

"Because this town is full of pompous jackasses, and I have a career to think about." She paused. "You want to know about Rory Allen?"

"Look who's changing the subject now."

"Rory is a non-starter. He doesn't have the resources to alter autopsy reports."

"Who does? Desmond Ross?"

"Everyone has a price, and Desmond's got the financial means to tempt just about anyone. He's well connected. He had motive. He's certainly on my list of possibilities."

"Desmond pays Bhodi to sell Mia tainted drugs to avoid a scandal, then bribes someone in the lab or in the medical examiners' office," I postulated.

Lyric shrugged. "Stranger things have happened in this town."

She took a sip of her whiskey and casually glanced across the bar. Judging by the distasteful look that curled on her face, she saw something she didn't like. A groan escaped her pretty lips, "Good Lord."

"re you good at improv?" Lyric asked, smiling through gritted teeth as she waved to someone across the bar.

"What?" I asked.

"Go along with it and follow my lead."

Lyric put on a cheery face as a man strutted toward the table with a blonde on either arm.

His companions had model good looks. Long legs, fitted dresses, and sparkling jewelry. Low-cut necklines and high hemlines. Toned thighs. Impeccable bone structure.

"Lyric, funny seeing you here," the man said.

He and Lyric both smiled at each other, but their eyes filled with disdain. Invisible beams of hatred shot between them, each probably trying to incinerate the other with their minds.

The man was well dressed—a fashionable gray suit, white

shirt, silver tie, and matching pocket square. His brown hair was coiffed to perfection. The gold *Leroux* watch on his wrist was pricey.

Lyric's eyes flicked between the two blondes. The man displayed his companions proudly.

"Just having a few drinks," Lyric said.

"I didn't think this place was your style."

"Brock, I'd like you to meet Tyson Wild." Lyric grabbed my hand across the table, making sure Brock noticed the gesture. "Tyson, this is Brock Dorian."

I shook the man's hand.

"It's a pleasure to meet you," Brock said. He introduced his two companions. "This is Anoushka and Oksana."

There were smiles and handshakes all around.

"So, is this a first date?" Brock asked, smugly, trying not to sound too interested.

A fake laugh erupted from Lyric's lips. "No. We've been seeing each other for a while now. But every time seems like the first time. Right, honey?" Lyric squeezed my hand affectionately.

"Always a new discovery," I said.

Brock forced a smile. "Well, I don't want to interrupt your evening any more than I already have." His attention turned to Lyric. "I just wanted to say hello. I'm glad you're getting out. Moving on." Brock had a smug, condescending tone.

Lyric forced another smile.

Brock strolled away with the two beauties and made a point to let his hands slip down the smalls of their backs and grab handfuls of pert cheeks, goosing the girls.

Lyric groaned. "I hate that man. He's not even a man, he's a worm. A very small worm."

"I take it that was the pompous asshole?"

"The most recent one."

"So, you're telling me you have bad taste in men."

"I'm here with you, aren't I?"

"I thought this was just business."

"It is," she said, still holding my hand. Her hand was warm and soft. I didn't mind holding it.

"Think he bought it?" Lyric asked.

"Bought what?" I asked, knowing what she was referring to.

"You and me. It's not an outrageous pairing, is it?"

I shrugged. "Do you care?"

"Not really."

"Obviously, you do."

Her eyes narrowed at me. She glanced at Brock and his companions at the bar, ordering shots. "He's just a dick. That's all. And I don't want him to think I'm moping around, pining for him."

"Are you?"

Her eyes narrowed at me. "Do I look like I'm pining over anyone?"

I shrugged.

She sneered at me playfully.

Lyric glanced back to the bar, and her face crinkled. "Oh, my God. Seriously?"

Brock had locked lips with Oksana. They were exploring each other's tonsils with their tongues. His lips broke away from the Russian beauty, and he turned his attention to Anoushka. Their lips collided with a generous display of public affection.

"He's just doing this to get a rise out of me," Lyric said.

"Seems like it's working."

She glared at me. "It's not working."

Lyric glanced around the bar. "Where's our waitress? I think it's time for another drink."

Our server was nowhere in sight.

Lyric stood up, still holding my hand, and pulled me toward the bar. "Come on. Let's get a drink."

I tugged back against her hand. "I think this is a bad idea."

Her face scrunched. "Don't worry. I'm nowhere near my limit."

"That's not what I meant."

She tugged me toward the bar, closer to Brock. We leaned against the counter, and she flagged the bartender down. "Two shots of Jägermeister."

The bartender grabbed the bottle from the freezer and served up two of the syrupy brown shots.

"Put it on Mr. Wild's tab," Lyric said with a grin. She lifted the shot glass. "What should we toast too?"

"Poor life choices?"

"I'm on board with that. In the end, you will regret the things you didn't do more than the things you did," she said.

We clinked glasses and downed the minty licorice-like beverage. We both slammed the empty shot glasses on the counter, and I saw Lyric's eyes flick to Brock. He was watching us with curiosity, trying to be discreet about it.

Lyric moved close. I felt a tingle down my spine. Being in close proximity to a woman *that* beautiful was always something special. She put her hand on the back of my neck and pulled my face toward hers. Our lips collided, and our tongues danced.

She was just doing it to piss off Brock. I didn't mind. I didn't mind at all.

19

Her pillowy soft lips felt heavenly, and her slick tongue teased. Her warm body pressed against mine, igniting lustful thoughts. My hands traced the supple curves of her body.

We were all over each other at the bar. It was late enough, and most people were drunk enough, that it didn't draw much attention.

Brock put on a show with his two Russian beauties.

I was an innocent pawn in a jealous war. Sometimes you have to make sacrifices. War is hell.

It didn't take long for Lyric to say, "Let's get out of here."

Her delicate words tickled my ear and sent a spark of desire through my body.

Who was I to say no?

I settled the tab, and Lyric grabbed my hand, pulling me out of the bar, intentionally brushing past Brock and his entourage.

We crossed the lobby and hit the call button to the elevator. The doors slid open, and we stepped on.

Alone.

Within seconds, I had Lyric pinned against the wall, our mouths colliding, our bodies mashing against each other. My hands found every curve and valley. Somehow I managed to press the button for the 4th floor.

The elevator ride was too short. The bell rang, and the door slid open.

Someone cleared their throat, waiting to board the elevator.

After a moment, we broke free and came up for air. I looked at the gentleman waiting to step aboard. I recognized his face—a big-time movie star.

I grabbed Lyric's hand and pulled her off the elevator. The movie star grinned, stepped aboard the lift, and the doors slid shut.

"Was that...?" Lyric asked.

"Yes. I think it was."

I pulled her down the corridor, looking for my room number. We quickly realized we were on the wrong floor.

Whoops!

At the end of the hall, we pushed into the stairwell, and we found ourselves in another embrace.

Fuck it!

The stairwell was as good as the elevator.

We went at it hot and heavy for a few moments. Our hands groping and kneading each other's flesh. I spun her around, pushed her against the wall, and kissed the back of her neck. She jutted her sweet cheeks against my hips. My heart pounded, and blood swelled. My body burned with desire.

Hers did too. Heat radiated from her like a furnace.

It didn't take long before I hiked up her skirt and pulled her frilly lace panties down.

This was the Château, after all. We couldn't have been the first to christen the stairwell.

Moans of ecstasy echoed through the staircase. I'm sure it permeated every floor and spilled out into the lobby.

I didn't care if somebody walked in on us or not.

We worked up a sweat in the stairwell, then decided to take the party back to my hotel room. We hit the desk, knocking stationery and pens to the floor. After a moment, we moved to the balcony, letting our symphony of delight echo across the courtyard, bouncing across the water.

I wasn't sure if this was the kind of behavior that would get us kicked out of the hotel, or earn us reward points?

We finally ended up in bed, exhausted. I passed out with Lyric's smooth body wrapped around mine.

I woke the next morning with a phone call from JD, the sun beaming through gaps in the curtains. "Wake up, sleepyhead!"

I rubbed the sleep from my eyes. "I'm up," I yawned. "When are you coming out?"

"I'm here, bitch. Took the redeye."

"Why didn't you tell me? I could have sent the driver."

"I'm in a Zoomber." It was an upscale ride-sharing service. "I'll be there momentarily. What room are you in?"

"Number 421."

"Did you get a suite, or do I have to sleep on that shitty foldout couch?"

"Relax, I booked a suite. You've got your own bedroom."

"Good deal. See you in a few."

By the time the call ended, Lyric had already slipped out of bed. She disappeared into the bathroom. I heard the shower nozzle twist, and the spray hit the tile.

I grabbed the room service menu and looked over my breakfast options. The spinach and cheese omelette sounded good.

Lyric slipped out of the shower a few minutes later, wearing a fluffy white robe and a towel wrapped around her hair.

"I'm about to order room service. You want breakfast?"

"No, thank you," she said. "I'm late for work."

She peeled out of the robe, and I took the opportunity to survey her perfect form. She slipped on the skimpy blue cocktail dress from the night before, searched for her panties, shimmied them up her legs, then put on her high heels. Once she was put together, she marched to the bed, gave me a kiss, her wet hair dangling in my face. "I had fun. Maybe we can do it again sometime?"

"Maybe," I teased.

She gave me another kiss, then darted toward the door. "Walk of shame, here I come."

With that, she was gone.

I finally decided to climb out of bed. I took a shower, brushed my teeth, and ordered breakfast.

Room service arrived 20 minutes later.

The attendant rolled the cart into the room and served the meal. I put cash in his hand, and he left me to enjoy my breakfast.

Afterward, I texted David to touch base. He said he was putting the final touches on the treatment, and he would be in touch later for me to review. He asked me once again for my journals.

Lyric had given me the number to Amber Angel's agent. I thought it might be worth a quick call to see if I could pry out her personal contact information. A gruff, New York voice answered the phone when I called. "What do you need?"

"My name is Deputy Tyson Wild. I'm trying to get in touch with Amber Angel—real name Devon Scott. Can you give me her contact info?"

20

"Nice try, pal. You and everybody else want a piece of that," the voice said.

"This is official police business," I assured. "I'm investigating a death."

"Yeah, and I'm the Pope. Give it a rest. Do like everybody else does. Buy one of her videos and jerk off."

He hung up the phone before I could protest further.

There was a knock at the door. When I pulled it open, JD was standing in the hall with a bellhop carrying his bags.

JD strutted into the room with a wide grin on his face.

The bellboy followed behind. "Where would you like your bags, sir?"

I said, "Put them in the bedroom on the right."

"Yes, sir," the bellboy said as he lugged JDs baggage into the other bedroom.

"What? No breakfast for me?" JD complained.

"Order some up."

JD tipped the bellboy before he left.

"Where exactly is the band staying when they get here?" I asked.

He looked at me like it was an idiotic question. "I told them to bring sleeping bags. They can crash on the floor. They're young. They can handle it. They can fight over the pullout bed."

I sighed and shook my head. "Why don't you spring for a room for them. You can afford it."

"I'm not paying for them to trash a hotel room at the Château and live out their rock 'n' roll fantasies."

"Aren't you living out your rock 'n' roll fantasies?"

"Yes, but I've earned it."

"Don't be a cheap ass, get them another room," I said. "You know this is going to turn into one long party."

Jack grinned. "I know. That's the fun of it. It's like an adventure that we're all taking together. We will have bonded by the end of this period, and we will have stories to tell that will last generations."

I rolled my eyes.

"How are the story meetings going?"

"Great. I think we're almost done."

JD smiled. "What about casting? Because I want approval on who plays me in the TV show. I've got a list."

"Save it for the meeting with the studio." JD was not getting approval on casting.

"What about Mia?"

I caught him up to speed on my investigation.

JD sniffed the air. Among the lingering scent of breakfast, the air swirled with coffee and the faint traces of Lyric's perfume. "Did you have company last night?"

"Yes, I did."

A sly smile curled his face. "I guess the investigation is going rather well, indeed."

"It has turned up some interesting surprises."

JD surveyed the accommodations, pacing around the suite. There was a palpable excitement in his eyes. "This is going to be great. We are going to totally rock that club come Friday night." He continued to survey the accommodations. "We have to honor the history of this establishment."

And by honor it, he meant throwing a party that was worthy of rock legends. The walls of the hotel kept the secrets of the icons of rock from the '60s, '70s, and '80s. JD wanted his band, *Wild Fury*, to be a part of that storied history.

He ambled to the house phone, dialed room service, and ordered breakfast. When he hung up the phone, he asked, "What are your plans for the day?"

I shrugged. "Trying to get in touch with Amber Angel."

His eyes lit up. "Oooh, Amber Angel. She's one of my favorites."

I told him about my failed attempt with her agent.

His face twisted. "Amateur. There's a simple solution for that. What's the number?"

I told him, and he dialed the agent. Through the tiny speaker, I heard the gruff voice bark.

"Hi," JD said. "I'm over at the Château in the middle of production, and one of our girls flaked out. We'd like to replace her with Amber Angel. Is she available today?" JD listened intently. "Yes, I'm sure she is in high demand."

The gruff voice crackled through the phone.

"Solo girl…. Yes, with toys." JD grinned. "If you need references, you can check my website." Jack gave him the address to his photography site. He looked at his watch. "1 PM would be great. Do you take credit cards?"

The gruff voice said something.

"Excellent. Let me give you the number. What's my total, with agency fee?"

21

"See," JD said with a beaming smile. "Easy as pie."

"Amber's going to be pretty upset when she gets over here and there's no actual job," I said.

"She's getting paid either way. And she doesn't have to sleep with some troll. It's a win-win."

"That seemed all too easy for you," I said. "Done that before?"

JD scowled at me. "It's just a business transaction. Plus, I ordered the cheapest option. As a solo act, she's not going to have to interact with other performers. That way, there's no need for testing or any of the usual hoops. We just need to check her ID, and I've got model releases in my bag."

"We're just asking her questions."

"You're just asking her questions. If I'm paying for it, I might as well take pictures."

"What happened to Sloan?"

"I'm not dead."

"You might be if Sloan finds out."

"There's nothing wrong with taking artistic, black-and-white photos of a beautiful woman. Besides, if you keep your trap shut, who's gonna know?"

I raised my hands in surrender. "You know I can keep a secret."

JD was merely in pursuit of Sloan. It was far from a done deal. A lunch date and a few pecks on the cheek hardly made a relationship. It was somewhat refreshing to know that JD hadn't totally changed his ways. I was beginning to worry that he had put all his eggs into one basket prematurely. From what I could tell, he sure was lovesick over Sloan. Who wouldn't be? She was a great woman. But she had expressed mild interest at best. I hoped it would work out for him.

We lounged by the pool for a while, had burgers for lunch, then made our way back up to the room in anticipation of our guest.

A few minutes before 1 PM, there was a knock on the door.

JD pulled it open with an eager smile. The sultry blonde little vixen stood in the hallway wearing sweats and holding a duffel bag. "Are you JD?"

"I am. Come on in."

He motioned for her to enter, and she stepped into the foyer. Her skeptical eyes surveyed the accommodations, then fell on me. "Is he talent?"

"No, he's my co-producer." JD looked at me and winked.

I waved at Amber.

"Where's makeup and the crew?"

"It's just us today," JD said. "Are you comfortable doing your own makeup?"

"Yeah, sure. Whatever. This is just *Solo Girl* stuff, right? I mean, I'll need to see his health card if you want me to fuck him," she said, pointing to me.

"Just solo stuff," JD assured.

"Okay. I brought an assortment of toys." She set the duffel bag on a table and unzipped it. She spread it open, and JD peered into the bag of naughty items. He looked shocked. I rarely saw anything that shocked JD.

She pulled out a gargantuan silicone pleasure device. The thing would make an elephant feel insecure in comparison. "This is the largest I can take. And if it goes up my ass, it's gonna cost double."

I almost choked. "We just want to ask you some questions."

"You mean, like pre-interview questions? Or questions on camera? What's the setup?"

I flashed my badge.

"Oh, so you're going to play a cop. What are you going to do? Catch me playing with myself and punish me?" She thought about it for a moment, then her face crinkled with confusion. She eyed JD. "I thought you said this was *Solo Girl*?"

"It is," I assured. "I'm really a cop. I want to ask you some questions about Mia Sophia."

Amber shifted uncomfortably.

"Don't worry, you're still going to get paid."

"You want me to talk about Mia on camera?"

"No. Off-camera."

Amber wasn't a brain surgeon.

"Okay. What do you want to know?"

"You worked for Nikki Griffin at the same time Mia did, right?"

She hesitated for a long moment. "Yeah. What's this about?"

"You know Mia is dead, right?"

"Duh. I'm not stupid."

"Was Desmond Ross ever a client?"

"That's how Mia met him. Nikki sent both of us to his hotel room one night. I could tell he liked Mia more than me. Which was just fine. That guy is gross. He stinks." Her pretty little nose crinkled.

"Did Mia continue to see Desmond after that?"

"Yeah. He would call Nikki and request Mia all the time."

"Do you know why Mia quit working for Nikki?"

"I think it wasn't for her. Getting busted didn't help either."

My brow lifted with surprise. "She got busted?"

"That's what I heard. Nikki sent her to a gig, and it got raided, or something like that. I never got the full story."

"Do you know if she got arrested?"

"I don't know. I'm just glad it wasn't me. That's another thing I like about adult films. It's not illegal in California. As long as there's a camera rolling, you can pay me for sex."

JD grinned.

According to the law, if you paid for sexual services, it was illegal. But if you were paying someone to have sex on camera for commercial entertainment, it was legal in the state of California. One of the only states in the union with such a loophole—which is why the San Fernando Valley is the adult entertainment capital of the world. The dirty little secret of Hollywood is that 75% of entertainment revenue comes from the adult industry. More than the biggest block-busters combined. Everything from camera rental, catering, crew personnel, editing, post production, and distribution. It also accounts for 75% of all online traffic. The city, county, and state liked the tax revenue too much to shut the whole thing down.

"What happened after Mia quit working for Nikki?" I asked.

Amber shrugged. "I don't really know. We lost touch. I tried to call her a few times, but she would never return my call."

"Can you think of anybody who wanted to harm Mia?"

She shrugged again. "Like I said, we weren't that close. We did a few gigs together. We did girl/girl stuff at parties for rich creeps."

"Why did you leave?"

"Nikki takes a larger cut than my current agent does. Doing on-camera stuff, I'm in control of my career. I say who I have sex with and who I don't. I get to build my brand, and I can tour around the country as a featured dancer at strip clubs and make a ton of money. And that money goes straight into my pocket."

I exchanged a glance with JD. I wanted to know more about Mia's arrest.

22

"Is that art, or is that art?" JD asked, showing me images he had taken of Amber on his phone.

They were tasteful shots.

Amber stepped out of his bedroom, wearing sweats, her duffel bag dangling from her shoulder. She gave JD a hug on the way toward the door. "Thanks again, guys. You were great to work with. Book me anytime."

JD smiled. "Thank you."

She slipped out of the room and pulled the door shut behind her.

"I think I'm in the wrong business," Jack said.

I gave him a look.

He shrugged innocently. "What? I just took a few pictures. Harmless fun. I didn't do anything with her, I swear."

"You better hope Sloan doesn't see those pictures, just saying."

He shook his head, dismissively. "It's fine art. I'm a fine art photographer."

I chuckled. "If you say so."

My phone buzzed with a call from David. "Hey, you got a minute?"

"Sure, what do you need?"

"I just want you to look over this treatment one last time before I finalize everything. And I use the term finalize loosely. This will be a work in progress until we begin production on the show."

I told David we'd meet him in the lobby in a few minutes. Then I called Isabella. "I need you to run a background check on Mia Sophia. Real name Mary Jane Burnett. I'm looking specifically for any history of an arrest record."

"Give me a minute, and I'll see what I can find out. I'll get back with you in a few."

I ended the call and slipped the phone back into my pocket.

"Something tells me you're not going to find an arrest record," JD said. "It would have been all over the tabloids."

"Agreed," I said. "I need to talk to Nikki Griffin. See if there's any truth to what Amber said."

A moment later, a text dinged back from Isabella. *[No criminal history. Just a few parking and speeding tickets.]*

[Thanks.]

"It's possible her record could have been expunged," JD said.

"There would still be a record of the arrest."

"Not if a few wheels were greased. You don't stay in business hustling high-end hookers without having law enforcement on the payroll."

"You think Nikki Griffin has someone on the payroll?"

"No doubt about it. I suppose Desmond could grease the wheels if he didn't want his up-and-coming starlet outed as a former prostitute. Maybe that's part of the leverage he had over her. Maybe she wanted out from under his thumb and threatened to expose him. They both would go down in flames if they turned on each other, but maybe Mia thought she could come out looking like the victim? A good publicist might be able to spin it."

I needed one more favor from Isabella. I texted her Nikki Griffin's number and asked her to locate her cell phone. She texted back a few minutes later with an address in Malibu. I planned to pay Nikki a visit after my meeting with David.

David was in the lobby when we arrived. We greeted each other and took a seat on the comfy couches. He had compiled all of his notes and typed them up into a presentable format. He handed me the small packet. The first page was a basic summary of the series, followed by character descriptions, then bullet point outlines for the first 12 episodes. It was just the basic skeleton of what the show could become.

I thumbed through it, made a couple of notes, then handed it to JD. His face crinkled when his eyes fell on the character descriptions. "Houston, we have a problem!"

David's face tensed with concern. "What's wrong?"

JD read the character description aloud. "*The quirky, but lovable, sidekick. Well past his prime, desperately hanging onto 29—an age he hasn't seen in decades. A walking, talking midlife crisis.*"

There was an uncomfortable silence.

Jack cleared his throat. "First of all, I am *lovable,* I have to admit. I don't know if I'd described myself as *quirky,* but certainly not *well past my prime.* The only 29 I'm hanging onto is a gorgeous brunette, and to be honest, she's closer to 26. And there is no *crisis.* I'm at my peak. And I'm having the time of my life."

David smiled. "No problem. That can be fixed with a couple of keystrokes."

Jack handed the treatment back to David with an annoyed frown. "And I'm thinking Brad Cruise should play me."

Brad Cruise was one of the biggest movie stars on the planet. The guy had six-pack abs, sparkling eyes, and a winning smile that could charm the pants off just about every woman he crossed paths with. Panties melted at the mere mention of his name, and girls swooned.

He was also getting $20 million a picture.

"Food for thought," David said, placating Jack. "We can discuss that in greater detail when we get to casting."

"I have one more suggestion, if I may," I said. "You might want to change the word *quirky* to *delusional.* Delusional sidekick."

Jack scowled at me.

fter the meeting with David, I called my agent, Joel. "Can you get me a meeting with Desmond Ross?"

"I can get you a meeting with anybody in this town," Joel said with confidence.

I had no doubt that he could.

"But why?"

"He seems like an industry player. I thought it might be a good idea to set up a general meet and greet."

Joel could see through my bullshit. "What are you up to?"

"Do I always have to be up to something?"

"I know you too well." Joel paused. "This isn't about Mia Sophia, is it?"

"It could be," I said innocently.

"You want me to set up a meeting with one of the most

powerful and influential men in Hollywood so you can harass him about the death of a starlet which you have no factual basis to connect him with?"

"Pretty much."

"Not to mention, you have no jurisdiction here."

"I don't think the truth cares about jurisdiction."

Joel sighed. "Of all my clients, you're one of my favorites, Tyson. You know that."

"Thank you. Of all my agents, you're one of my favorites, too," I mocked.

"And as your agent, I have a fiduciary duty to look out for your best interest. Setting up a meeting so you can harass Desmond Ross is not in your best interest, nor is it in mine."

"So, you won't set up the meeting?"

"Not only *no*, but *hell no!*"

"What if I want to find another agent who will?" I said, throwing it out there casually.

He scoffed. "Go ahead. I'll even help you find other representation if that's what you want. But as soon as they hear that you want to piss your career away and alienate everyone in the business, you'll get dropped. I don't think you want to be without an agent."

I had no desire to get into an argument with Joel. "Point taken. I wouldn't go looking for another agent anyway."

"I know. Once you've had the best, why mess with the rest?"

I chuckled.

"Do me a favor, leave Desmond Ross alone," Joel pleaded.

"What if he had Mia killed?"

"Do you really believe that?"

"I don't know what to believe. But I don't think Mia drowned in that pool all by herself. She had some assistance." I told him about the fentanyl, the alleged changeup of the autopsy report, and various rumors I had gathered.

"It's all weak, Tyson. Find something more substantial. When you've got something solid, bring it to the LAPD. They can take it to the District Attorney, and he can decide to move forward or not. Let them take the brunt of it. Nothing will blow back on you."

I paused for a moment. "I promise I will stay out of trouble."

"I don't believe your promises, but that's what I'm going to go with right now to keep my anxiety level low. How's it going with David?"

"I read his final treatment today. So far, so good."

"I'll set up a meeting with Susan. You and David can go over what you've come up with and get her to sign off on everything."

"Then what?"

"Then, David will do what a producer does. Hire the creative team—directors, writers, crew. Once everything is green-lit, pre-production will ramp up. I'll let you know when I have the meeting arranged."

He cautioned me again before hanging up.

We took a Zoomber to El Toro Beach in Malibu. Nikki

Griffin had a home in a gated community. There was no way we were going to pull up to the gate in a Zoomber and gain access pretending to be LA County. But there was a public beach access point less than 500 yards away.

We had the Zoomber driver drop us off at the parking lot, and we took the meandering wooden steps down to the magnificent beach.

Blue waves crashed against the sand. Stunning rock formations protruded from the sea and along the shore. One particular formation created an archway of stone. There were several professional photographers snapping photos of bikini-clad models against the rocks.

Toned bodies glistened in the sun, and grains of sand stuck to pert assets. Seabirds hung in the air, and pelicans gathered on the rocks. Whitewater crashed against the stone formations, and the smell of salt water filled my nostrils. It reminded me of Coconut Key, and how much I missed the place—even though I'd only been gone a few days.

We walked along the beach, southward. There was a *no trespassing* sign where the private homes began. The sign referenced a list of state statutes. Malibu was notorious for overzealous homeowners and their attempts to keep the public off their beaches. But according to the Coastal Waters Act of 1972, all beaches south of the mean high-tide line were public—much to the chagrin of the wealthy tech billionaires and movie moguls who bought up all of the prime real estate.

Malibu was loaded with fake *no parking* signs and misleading signs near public access gates stating *passage by permission of owner only*. Some owners had even gone to the lengths of locking public access gates, barricading ease-ments, and embarking on misinformation campaigns.

It was no wonder people in California hated the rich. Quite a few of them acted like assholes.

There were six houses along the beach that backed up to the white sand. Beyond that, sheer cliffs towered over the beach. Luxurious homes sat perched on the edge with precarious walkways down to the shore.

The large, modern three-story home on the beach belonged to Nikki Griffin. It looked like it could have been the set of a movie. It probably had been at some point—certainly a few adult films.

The home was L-shaped, and large windows blended indoor and outdoor spaces. The structure wrapped around the pool that was landscaped with palm trees and a swim-up bar. Gorgeous beauties sunned themselves on lounges by the pool. These were no doubt Nikki's girls.

A stairway led down from the patio to the beach. The gate guarding the steps was unlocked.

We climbed the staircase, emerging poolside, acting like we belonged there.

The act didn't last long.

A blonde with ringlets and oversized sunglasses barked at us, "Who the fuck are you?"

24

The blonde was upset. She had every right to be. She sat up in the lounge chair on her elbows, sunscreen and sweat beading on her tanned skin. She had a flat stomach, and the seams of her bikini screamed for mercy against her shapely endowments. She was mid-30s, but her body was indiscernible from the 22-year-olds lounging around her.

This had to be Nikki Griffin.

The angry blonde shouted, "Quinton!"

I had no doubt in my mind that Quinton was her muscle. I flashed my badge, trying to defuse the situation. "Deputy Wild. We spoke on the phone."

She snarled at me. "And I told you I had nothing to say. You're trespassing. Leave now, before I have you thrown in jail."

Quinton stormed from the house, marching around the pool. A quick glance told me he wasn't anyone I wanted to mess with. The sun glared off his bald head. The dark sport-sunglasses he wore concealed his eyes. His body was thick and round, and his head disappeared into his beefy shoulders. "Is there a problem here?"

"No problem," I said. "Just asking the lady some questions."

"I don't think the lady wants to answer them."

"Get him out of here," Nikki commanded.

Quinton reached to grab my arm.

I jerked away. "I'm leaving."

I took a step back and raised my hands innocently as Quinton kept pushing toward me.

"If you want my advice, Deputy," Nikki said, "go back to wherever it is you came from. You have no idea what you're getting yourself into."

"I was hoping you could tell me."

Quinton was a wall of meat pushing towards us. JD and I maneuvered to the stairs and made our way down the beach.

Quinton followed along, locking the gate behind us. "Everything above the high water line is private property. I will call the police if you don't get walking."

"Good to see you, too! Have a nice afternoon," I said, my voice thick with sarcasm.

We headed back to the public area, plodding through the soft sand, listening to the gulls squawk overhead and the waves crash against the shore.

"What do you think she's hiding?" JD asked.

"I'd sure like to know."

We walked down the beach and watched a photographer shoot models for a moment. Then we climbed the steps up the hillside to the parking lot. I called for a Zoomber, and we made the twenty-mile drive down PCH to West Hollywood. It was a little too late to stop by Desmond Ross's office in Santa Monica and poke the bear.

The sun hung low over the water, and the sky filled with glorious amber light. The kind of light that made Los Angeles famous. It was the ideal time of day to have a photoshoot or film a movie scene—known as *magic hour*—that limited window of time where the universe provided the quality of light you just couldn't match with any type of synthetic lighting.

By the time we got back to the Château, I was starving. JD and I went up to the room, changed for the evening, and headed back down to the restaurant. There were tons of great places to eat in LA, but I didn't want to take the time to pick one out, get seated, and wait to be served. Besides, the food wasn't bad in the hotel.

The hostess seated us at a table in the corner. A waitress swung by, introduced herself, delivered glasses of water, and asked if we wanted any appetizers.

"Just give us a minute," JD said, looking over the menu.

"Absolutely, sir. I'll be back to check on you shortly."

I knew what I wanted, so I took the opportunity to text Bhodi Hendrix. It was about time I had a few words with the drug dealer. [In from out of town. Looking to party. Blaine sent me. Can you help?]

I hoped Zach wasn't lying and that using Blaine as a reference was valid.

I set the phone on the table and waited for a return. A few minutes later, the phone buzzed with a text from Bhodi. *[Blaine owes me money.]*

[Sounds like Blaine's problem, not mine.]

A minute went by with no response.

I texted again. [No worries. I guess I'll take my business elsewhere.]

The waitress returned to take our order. Jack ordered the linguini with clam sauce, and I opted for the steak frites again. Call me a creature of habit.

25

J ack's head was on a swivel, surveying the crowd. There were quite a few recognizable faces in the restaurant.

We were halfway through the meal when I got a text back from Bhodi. *[I'll be at Prism around 11 PM. What do you need?]*

[A ball.] It was a reference to an eight-ball (3.5 grams of cocaine).

[Don't waste my time.] The amount obviously wasn't enough for him.

[Who am I? Tony Montana?]

[That's exactly it. I don't know who you are.]

[I can do a half-zip. As long as it's glacial.] Slang for half an ounce, and pure as arctic ice.

There was another long pause.

[Never been stepped on.] It was an assurance the product

hadn't been cut. Half the stuff on the street was cut with substances that ranged from relatively harmless to extremely toxic—laxatives, laundry detergent, boric acid. Not stuff you really want to be putting up your nose. *[11 PM. Cash. No bullshit.]*

[$$$?]

[If you have to ask...]

[I'll be there.]

[Text me when you are in the club.]

A grin curled on my face.

"Got a hot date?" JD asked.

I frowned at him. "No. Just set up a drug buy. We're going to see what Bhodi knows."

We finished our meal and headed up to the room. We had time to kill before hitting *Prism,* and Jack poured himself a glass of whiskey. I hadn't told him the story about how I acquired the liquor.

"Want a drink?"

"Not yet."

JD's face crinkled.

"I want to stay sharp for the meeting with Bhodi."

"Suit yourself," Jack said, tipping back the glass.

After he was sufficiently lubricated, we left the hotel and hit the strip.

Prism was a techno club with booming base, swirling lights, and hordes of pretty people. Fog machines billowed smoke onto the dance floor, and spotlights slashed the hazy air. Strobe lights flickered.

I didn't want to blow our cover, so I didn't use my all-access pass. I kept the badge in my pocket. The line wasn't too bad, but the $40 cover was lame.

We mingled through the dense club, making our way to the bar. JD ordered a round of drinks, strictly to maintain our cover. I texted Bhodi. [We're here. Where are you?]

He buzzed back a moment later. *[I'm upstairs in the back, sitting on the couch underneath the fake Picasso.]*

[Be right there.]

I nudged JD, and we drifted through the club. We spiraled up the staircase and made our way around the upper floor. The center was cutaway, allowing a view of the dance floor below. The upstairs had a calmer, more chill vibe.

There were two smaller bars rimming the outer wall of the second floor. In the far corner there was a lounge area with couches and coffee tables.

There was a guy sitting on a couch under the fake Picasso with a couple of hotties—a brunette and a redhead. I assumed that was Bhodi.

He had shaggy blonde hair, wore a white dress shirt with a red rose pattern embroidered on the left breast and black slacks. The babes on either side wore tight dresses with high hemlines that accentuated their stunning legs.

"You Bhodi?" I asked as I approached.

"You Blaine's friend?"

I nodded.

He climbed off the couch and shook my hand, then shook JD's. He must have mistaken JD for the famous '80s rockstar. A wide grin curled on Bhodi's face. "Why didn't you tell me you were with the legend?"

JD grinned and went along with it.

"Big fan," Bhodi said. "You need a half zip, right?"

I nodded.

"Let's do this somewhere more private." He motioned for us to follow him.

Bhodi led us to a hallway by the bathrooms. The dark corridor was empty, not like the bathrooms downstairs that had lines around the corner.

I flashed a wad of cash. "Will this cover it?"

"And then some." Bhodi glanced around, then dug into his pocket. He pulled out half an ounce of cocaine in small baggies and slapped them into my hand. He snatched the cash and looked it over, counting it.

The flash of my shiny gold badge ruined the party. Bhodi didn't notice the fine print.

His eyes widened, and he launched into a sprint.

I grabbed him and slammed him against the wall.

JD grabbed the wad of cash from his hand.

"Mother fucker!" Bhodi grumbled. "See, this is why I don't do business with people I don't know." His eyes blazed into JD, still thinking he was the famous '80s rocker. "And what's your involvement in this? Are you guys fucking with me?"

"Nope," I said.

A snarl twisted his face. "This is bullshit. Talk to Paxton."

"Who's Paxton?" I asked.

"You know what, I'm not saying shit to you guys without a lawyer."

"You tell me what I want to know, I might consider letting you go, for a small fee."

His eyes narrowed at me. "You assholes are all the same."

"You sold drugs to Mia Sophia," I said.

"I didn't sell shit to nobody."

"You just sold half an ounce to me. I'm sure when the lab tests this it's going to turn out to be more than just baby laxative." I paused for effect. "We can do this the easy way or the hard way."

Bhodi's eyes burned into me.

He looked at JD. "Your music sucks, by the way."

"Start talking," I said.

"I'm not saying shit until I talk to Paxton. You're LA County, right? Don't you assholes talk?"

JD and I exchanged a curious glance.

"Yeah. We talk," I said, rolling with it.

"Then why are you fucking with me?"

"Because I want answers. So start talking. Did you sell Mia Sophia drugs?"

"Okay, yeah. Maybe I sold her something. I sell a lot of people something."

"Something laced with fentanyl?"

His face twisted. "What!?"

"I don't know if you've been keeping up with current events, but Mia Sophia died of a drug overdose."

"I thought she drowned."

"There was enough fentanyl in her system to kill a large elephant."

"She didn't get it from me. My shit is 100% *Grade A* pure. See for yourself."

"Oh, I intend to test this out," I said. "Do you know Desmond Ross?"

"I know a lot of people."

"You know, I have a theory," I said.

"I don't really give a shit."

"Oh, you will. You want to know what my theory is?"

"Not really."

"I think somebody paid you to sell bad drugs to Mia Sophia because they wanted her to keep her mouth shut. That sound familiar?"

"Sounds like you watch too much TV."

"Who is Paxton?"

"Fuck you both. You know what? Arrest me. See what happens."

"I bet you've got enough product on you to go away for the foreseeable future."

It was all bullshit. I had no jurisdiction.

Bhodi clammed up and just stared at me.

"Last chance," I said. "Are you sure there's nothing else you'd like to say?"

A flashlight blinded my eyes. A silhouetted figure shouted, "Is there a problem here?"

26

I couldn't see shit with the flashlight in my eyes. "I'm a police officer," I said, the beam drawing closer.

"LAPD. Let's see your badge," Mr. Flashlight said. He was holding a badge of his own.

I released Bhodi and flashed the shadowy figure my badge. He drew closer and examined it. "You're a long way from home."

He clicked off the flashlight, and it took a second for my eyes to adjust.

He was still holding his badge for me to see. The guy was in plain clothes—brown leather jacket, dress shirt, pants. I knew right away he was a detective. He had shaggy brown hair, a mustache, and a day's worth of stubble. There was a faded scar on his right brow and cheek, like someone had taken a broken bottle to his face during a bar fight at some point in the distant past.

"Beat it," the cop said to Bhodi.

I knew what was happening, but I decided to push the issue anyway. "I just busted him on a drug buy."

"Like I said, you are well out of your jurisdiction. And he's one of mine."

"A confidential informant?"

"Yes. And I don't appreciate you two dildos fucking with my CI."

I decided to take the political approach. "My apologies. I'm just trying to track down information."

"Information about what?"

His eyes flicked to JD. "Hey, aren't you...?"

JD decided to play it straight. "No. But I get that all the time."

"What kind of information do you need?" the detective asked.

"You just let that guy sell cocaine in the club with impunity?" I asked.

"It's a cost of doing business. I let him do his thing, he rats out bigger dealers that come along. You know how it works."

I nodded. "It just sucks that scumbags like that get a free pass."

"So I can bust bigger scumbags." He redirected the conversation. "Why are you messing with my CI?"

"You're Paxton?" I asked.

"Yeah, who are you? And why are you here?"

"Mia Sophia's mother asked me to look into her death."

"There's nothing to look into," he said. "And you're way out of your territory. I don't like people stepping on my toes. How would you feel if I came down to wherever it is you're from and started snooping around?"

"I can't say that I'd like it."

"Well, now that we understand each other." Paxton looked us over. He stared at JD for a long moment, still confused by his resemblance. "What makes you think Mia's death wasn't accidental?"

I told him about the fentanyl.

"I read the autopsy report. It didn't say anything about fentanyl," Paxton said.

"I have sources that say different."

He shook his head and sighed. "Then, your sources are wrong." He looked perturbed. "Who are these *sources*?"

"I can't say exactly. They come from a trusted source."

He looked at me incredulously, lifting his brow. "So, you heard it from a friend, who heard it from a friend, who heard it from a friend? That might pass for police work down in the Keys. But it doesn't fly here."

"Just following the leads," I said.

He surveyed us for a long moment. "Look, if there's anything I can do to help you two out, call me. But don't go doing things on your own without approval. You got it?"

I nodded. "Fair enough."

Paxton handed me his card. "I'll look into this autopsy report thing for you. If something looks funny, I'll let you know. How do I get in touch with you?"

I gave him my number and handed him the bag of cocaine I had taken from his informant.

We left the club and stepped onto the sidewalk. Cars buzzed up and down Sunset.

"Well, he was a nice guy," JD said in a sardonic tone.

"I wouldn't like somebody messing with one of our informants either," I said. "But I sure would like to see Bhodi get his ass nailed. A guy like that belongs behind bars."

"I have no doubt that guy will get what's coming to him," JD said. "It just may take longer than either of us would like."

"When I brought up the fentanyl with Bhodi, I could see in his eyes that he didn't know what I was talking about."

"It happens," JD said with a shrug. "Sometimes somebody down the road cuts the product, and you don't know what's in it." JD started walking west down the sidewalk. "Come on. I want to show you something."

"Where are we going?"

A sly smile curled on JD's face. "You'll see."

We walked downhill, past bars, restaurants, outdoor cafés, and adult novelty stores. It didn't take long for me to figure out where we were going.

I texted Isabella along the way and asked her to send me background information on Detective Paxton. I wanted to make sure he was on the up and up.

It's not unusual for a confidential informant to get a pass as long as he keeps the officers in the loop and provides a constant stream of fresh busts. Departments like the process because it keeps their arrest record high. Good numbers mean they're doing their job. It lets the politicians point to a statistic and say, "See. We are tough on crime. The neighborhood is getting safer!"

Who knows? Maybe letting a small fish go to catch a bigger fish is in the best interest of the community. But rotten fish start to stink pretty damn quick. And Bhodi Hendrix was pretty rotten.

The pink and blue neon glow of *Girls Unlimited* bathed us as we passed by. The sultry neon outlines beckoned men into the den of iniquity.

"This is the place I was telling you about," I said.

JD gazed at the signage. "Looks like my kind of place. The band will love this. We'll have to party here one night."

I was surprised JD didn't want to immediately venture inside.

We kept heading west, past the *Serpent Room*—the intimate nightclub that had witnessed the demise of more than one celebrity icon. On the corner of San Torino and Sunset, JD motioned to the marquis above *Sour Mash*. Black letters spelled *Wild Fury, Fri. Nt.*

It was a sight to behold.

The name of Jack's band in lights, gracing the same marquee as countless other bands that had built the foundations of rock 'n' roll.

Jack soaked up the view with pride. He took a picture of the marquee. "The rest of the band's gonna be here tomorrow. I'm going to put their asses to work selling tickets. I want this to be a sold-out show. Standing room only."

"How are you going to do that?"

"I have ideas," he said with a devious grin.

27

"Let's go inside and check it out," JD said. "I want to get a feel for the place."

We crossed the street and strolled to the main entrance. Music from a live band spilled onto the sidewalk. JD nodded at the bouncer and marched in like he owned the place, his long blond hair flowing behind him. The bouncer clearly mistook him.

Inside, the crowd was thin. The band thrashed around on stage. They weren't very good.

Jack took a deep breath, trying to absorb the essence of the venue. "You can just feel the history in this place."

"The ghosts of rock 'n' roll past," I said in a slightly mocking tone.

Jack scowled at me.

He regarded the venue as stepping into a cathedral. A place of worship. A shrine to the gods of rock.

We moved to the bar, and Jack ordered us both a glass of whiskey. The bartender slid the drinks across the counter, and Jack paid the tab. I think the bartender would have given us the drinks free. In this venue, and the dim light, Jack's resemblance was remarkable.

"Looking good," the bartender said. "Have you lost weight?"

Jack smiled, playing along. "I have, and thank you for noticing."

JD had been keeping himself fit in the wake of our bet.

We mingled through the club and searched for local talent. Though his mind was preoccupied with Sloan, it didn't keep JD from looking for a good view. But the band on stage didn't have much draw, and it was slim pickings among the groupies.

After a few songs, JD had his fill.

We left *Sour Mash* and headed east on Sunset, back toward the hotel. There was still a good hour left until closing time. More than enough time to get into trouble at the hotel bar. We hadn't traveled more than a few steps when JD pointed up to a billboard that loomed above the boulevard.

My jaw dropped, and my brow lifted in surprise. "I don't even want to know what that cost you."

JD shrugged and smiled. "Sometimes you've got to spend money to make money."

The billboard featured *Wild Fury* in full '80s get up, looking like glam rockers. Teased hair, eyeliner, bandanas, studded bracelets, and lots of leather. It listed the date of the show, and the venue, along with the band's website.

"Impressive," I said.

A text buzzed through on my phone. It was from Isabella. It contained images of Detective Paxton, along with his file.

I briefly glanced over it as we kept walking, my head buried in my phone. It seemed that Chuck Paxton was just your average, ordinary vice cop. He had shot a few people in the line of duty, but they were all deemed within departmental protocol. He was divorced and remarried. It's tough being a cop's wife. Especially a vice cop's wife. He'd served in the army, and had been on the job almost 15 years.

We made it back to the hotel and stopped in the bar for a drink. I had a few questions for Marcel, but he wasn't working this evening.

There was a good size crowd, but not shoulder to shoulder. We were probably only there 15 minutes when I got a text from Lyric. *[I just got a disturbing phone call.]*

[What happened?]

[I hate to be that needy girl, but do you think you could come by my house? I'm a little freaked out.]

[Sure. Where do you live?]

She texted me the address.

I didn't think this was a dramatic ploy to get me to come see her in the middle of the night. And even if it was, I can't say that I totally minded.

"I gotta run," I told JD. "Something freaked Lyric out."

A quizzical look twisted on Jack's face.

"She's been getting threats. You going to be okay on your own?"

JD grinned. "I'll manage."

"Don't do anything Sloan wouldn't approve of," I teased.

He gave me a sour look.

I scheduled a Zoomber and left the bar. The driver whisked me up into the hills, winding through the canyon roads. We headed up Benedict Canyon, then turned into a neighborhood. The driver pulled to the curb at 10062 Hillview Drive.

I hopped out of the car and stepped onto the sidewalk. There was a brown slatted fence that surrounded the property. The two-story home was sleek and modern. It looked like it could have been designed by Frank Lloyd Wright or John Lautner. There was a mix of concrete and wood. Palm trees towered overhead, and foliage ensconced the house.

It was a nice place.

Either the reporters in this town made a lot of money, or Lyric had other sources of income.

We were just a few blocks away from Cielo Drive. The location of the infamous Manson murders. The original house had been bulldozed, and a new mansion was built in its place. I could see it from where I stood. Though the murders happened over 50 years ago, it still gave the place an eerie vibe. Every year, on the anniversary of the gruesome event, aficionados made the pilgrimage to the former residence and held candlelight vigils.

I walked up the driveway to Lyric's home and rang the bell. Her little red Ferrari was out front.

It was hard not to stare at the sharp lines of the exquisite car.

A few moments later, Lyric pulled open the door and ushered me inside with nervous eyes.

"What's going on?" I asked.

"I got a strange call. An ominous voice said *you were warned.* Then they hung up." She trembled with nerves. "Somebody knows I'm still digging into this case, and they don't like it." She paused. "Do you want a drink?"

I shook my head. "I've had enough."

"Thanks for coming. I'm glad you're here." She gave me a hug.

"No problem," I said, squeezing her back. I could feel her tremble.

She broke free, and I followed her into the open living area. Floor-to-ceiling windows offered a view of the backyard and the stunning swimming pool, which was illuminated with underwater lighting. The home was like a little oasis.

"This is a nice place," I said. "And that's a really nice car in the driveway."

"The perks of being a studio brat."

I arched a curious eyebrow.

She told me her dad was a big-time movie producer. She rattled off a list of hits that he had produced. He passed away a few years ago and left her with a sizable fortune.

"The news gig is what, like a hobby?" I asked.

"I'm not even going to begin to say it's tough growing up in the shadow of someone who was extremely successful. But it does set a high bar. I'm trying to make my own way in the world and to make a difference. But I also have a soft spot for Ferraris and fine architecture."

"How you spend your money is your business."

She smiled. "It is, isn't it?" She paused. "I feel a little embarrassed for dragging you all the way up here. Maybe it's not that big of a deal. But after my tires were slashed, I'm a little skittish."

"Don't be embarrassed. These people are obviously capable of murder. What time did the call come in?"

Lyric looked at her recent call list and told me the time.

I pulled out my phone and texted Isabella. I gave her Lyric's cell number and asked her to trace the call.

Isabella texted back a few moments later. *[Burner phone. Somewhere in West Hollywood. Benedict Canyon and Hillview Drive.]*

A wave of concern washed over my face.

"What's the matter?" Lyric asked.

"That call you got came from just around the corner."

I moved to the entrance foyer and peered out through the sidelights that framed the door. With concerned eyes, I surveyed the street.

My hand twisted the deadbolt. I pulled open the front door and marched down the driveway.

"Where are you going?" Lyric hissed in the doorway.

I reached the street and glanced in either direction—I didn't see anyone.

After a moment, I moved back to the house and shut the door behind me as I entered the foyer. Lyric twisted the deadbolt, and I moved through the house, securing the perimeter, peering out windows, scanning the backyard, assessing threats.

"You must have rattled somebody's cage," I said. "Who have you been talking to?"

28

"Oh, so this is *my* fault?" she asked with her hands on her sassy hips.

I chuckled. "No, it's not your fault. But if you can tell me which ant pile you've been poking, maybe we can figure out who's behind the threats."

"Whoever killed Mia Sophia is behind the threats," she said.

"We've established that," I said.

"Well, thank you, Mr. Detective. I'm glad you're on top of it."

"Is that why you called me over here, to get on top of it?" I asked, stepping toward her.

"No," she protested with a sparkle in her eyes. "I mean, if you were to insist..."

Our lips were inches apart. I reached my hand around and grabbed her by the small of her back, pulling her into me. Our mouths collided. We melted into one another, desire swelling.

After a pleasurable moment, we broke for a breath of air.

"I swear, I didn't invite you over with an ulterior motive," she said. "I really am concerned."

"Do you have a gun?"

Her face crinkled. "What? No. This is California."

"Do you know anything about Chuck Paxton? Vice detective, LAPD?"

She shook her head.

"I ran into him when I was investigating Bhodi Hendrix." I filled her in on the details.

"I don't care what Detective Paxton says, my source has never been wrong. If she says there were traces of fentanyl in Mia's blood, I believe her."

"Who is your source?"

Lyric shook her head. "No. I can't tell you. I will not violate that trust."

"Your source may be in danger. That's the most damning piece of evidence you've uncovered so far. A third-party report that conflicts with the official autopsy... that's troublesome for quite a few people."

Lyric squirmed uncomfortably for a moment. She bit her bottom lip and worry creased her face. "I'm only telling you this because I think you're right. My source is a forensic biochemist that works in said *third-party lab*. She's been a valuable source for a number of years. She's always spoken to me under the condition of anonymity. When you live in a town where celebrity overdoses are a common occurrence, it helps to have an inside source that can sort fact from fiction."

"She could lose her job for sharing that kind of information with you."

"Hence the reason I keep my sources secret."

"And how are you able to get this information?" I reconsidered the question. "On second thought, I don't want to know." I took a deep breath. "Call your source. Now!"

Lyric's brow lifted. "Now? It's almost 2 AM."

"I think your source deserves a heads-up."

She bit her lip again. "You're right."

Lyric pulled out her cell phone and dialed the number. It rang a few times and went straight to voicemail. "Hey, it's me. I know it's late. Call me as soon as you get this. I've been getting threats, and I think you might be in danger, too."

She ended the call and slipped the device back into her pocket.

"Where does the biochemist live?" I asked.

Her face twisted with a quizzical look. "Why? You want to go over to her place in the middle of the night?"

I nodded. "Yeah, I do."

Lyric hesitated for a moment. "Okay. I'll drive. She's just over the hill in the *Valley*."

Lyric grabbed the keys to the Ferrari, and we moved to the front door. I surveyed the driveway through the sidelights by the door—it looked clear.

My palm wrapped around the grip of my pistol, snatching it from its holster.

Lyric set the alarm to the house, and I pulled open the front door. The barrel of my pistol swept the area as I scanned for threats.

We hurried to the Ferrari, and I climbed into the passenger seat. The dash was black leather, and the bucket racing seats were Bordeaux red. The full-leather door panels were black and red, and there were generous helpings of carbon fiber and aluminum trim throughout the interior cabin. The GT-style steering wheel looked like it belonged in a race car, and the tachometer face was painted in racing yellow. The famous prancing horse of Ferrari adorned the center crest of the steering wheel. The air-conditioning vents looked like thrusters on an FA-18 super hornet. The fit and finish were second to none. Handcrafted perfection.

When Lyric cranked up the V12, it roared like a caged beast. With the press of a button, the hardtop roof folded away like some type of alien transformer. The 812 GTS looked like a rolling shark with aggressive lines and a front face that could eat anything on the road.

Lyric eased the car forward, angling the nose to just the right degree to get out of the driveway without scraping the aero-kit against the street. She gunned it once we were clear, and the acceleration thrust me against the bucket seats that fit like a glove.

The exhaust popped and rattled.

Lyric liked to drive fast.

This thing could carve up canyon roads like a serial killer

slicing through teens in a horror flick. We twisted through the hills, the exhaust note echoing through the canyon. The night air whipped around the cabin, and the gloomy glow of the night sky hovered above. The lights of the city made it too bright to see more than a few stars.

I figured JD would be envious. We didn't have twisty canyon roads back in Coconut Key. No place to push a precision automobile to its limits in quite the same way. One mistake here and you'd be into the side of the mountain or, perhaps, someone's pool.

We crested the ridge, wound our way down Mulholland, then made our descent into the San Fernando Valley. With every turn, the seat bolsters held my body in place, and the safety harness tightened around my hips and chest. This wasn't a wimpy four-cylinder turbo-hybrid. This was a V12 monster—ready, willing, and able to devour the road.

Lyric followed the instructions of the sat-nav, and with a few twists and turns, we pulled to the curb in front of the biochemist's house.

I climbed out of the low-slung car and closed the door behind me. My eyes scanned the area. I advanced up the walkway to the front door, and I already knew there was a problem.

29

T he home at 14555 Antelope Ridge was a midcentury modern one-story ranch style with elegant lines. The street was on an incline, and the front lawn was more of a mound than a yard. It was landscaped with robust foliage that could survive the dry months. A wispy Desert Willow presided over the smaller shrubs. There were frosted glass panels in the garage door. The stepped walkway, lined with concrete garden boxes, led to a recessed entryway. Wall sconces illuminated the area. They were the only lights on.

There were two tall double doors, though one of them was just for show. The functional door was slightly ajar.

Who leaves their door ajar at 2 AM in Los Angeles?

Nobody.

I drew my pistol and crept forward with caution.

The door was a modern design with multiple, narrow, horizontal panes of frosted glass. Someone had busted one of the panes, reached their hand inside, and twisted the deadbolt.

I nudged it open gently, and the hinges creaked. A sprinkling of frosted glass sparkled on the floor, catching the faint light from a streetlamp across the street.

The home was dark.

"Stay here," I said to Lyric.

Her worried eyes glanced around, surveying the area. I don't think she was too keen on being left on the porch alone. She also wasn't too keen on stepping into the dark house.

I used a small tactical flashlight on my keychain to illuminate the way. The shards of glass crunched under my feet as I stepped into the foyer, my pistol leading the charge.

Lyric hovered in the doorway, her head on a swivel.

The beam of my flashlight swept across the living room as I entered, illuminating the white leather couch, the glass coffee table, and the flatscreen display. In the hallway that led to a bedroom, the beam raked across a body.

I could only assume it was the biochemist.

She lay on the tile, lifeless. Her hair tousled, and her limbs contorted at an unnatural angle. Crimson blood pooled the tile around the body. There was no motion in her chest. She wasn't breathing. The biochemist was long dead.

I moved to the body, careful not to step in the pool of blood. I touched her skin with the back of my hand. The skin felt several degrees below normal.

I backed away and returned to the entrance.

Lyric's quizzical eyes surveyed me. I answered her gaze with a grim shake of my head.

"Oh, my God! What happened?"

"I don't know. She was shot twice. Call 911."

Lyric pulled out her phone, and her frantic fingers dialed 911. She stammered, "I'd like to report a homicide."

She gave the emergency operator the details and the address.

It took longer than you would think for the authorities to arrive.

An ambulance arrived first, followed by the red and blue lights of a patrol car. The EMTs assessed the situation and quickly determined there was nothing that could be done. The patrol officers secured the crime scene and waited for the medical examiner.

An officer asked us the standard questions.

A black, unmarked Dodge pulled to the curb, and Detective Paxton hopped out. He marched up the walkway and shook his head when he saw us. "You sure do get around, don't you?"

I shrugged.

"What are you doing here?"

"I was worried about my friend," Lyric said. "She didn't answer the phone when I called. We stopped by to make sure she was okay."

"You just happened to stop by in the middle of the night?" Paxton asked, incredulous.

"Like I said, I was worried about her."

"Why?"

"Call it *woman's intuition*."

"Don't go anywhere." Paxton stepped inside, the glass crunching under his shoes. He stepped into the living room and surveyed the gruesome scene.

Paxton returned to us a moment later. "Who is she?"

"Sidney Caldwell."

"You can positively ID her?" Paxton asked.

Lyric shrugged. "I didn't actually see the body." Her eyes flicked to me. "Tyson is the one who discovered her."

Paxton's suspicious eyes fell on me.

"We arrived at the home. There were signs of forced entry. I entered the house and discovered the body in the living room in the hallway. I checked for vitals. There were none. I left the house, and Lyric called 911."

"And what's your relationship to the deceased?" Paxton asked.

"I have no relationship."

"Never met her before in your life?"

"Nope."

"You just decided to escort Ms. Stone here in the middle of the night?"

"I didn't think Ms. Stone should be alone."

"I've been receiving threats," Lyric added.

"From whom?" Paxton asked.

"If I knew who was threatening me, I would have made a police report," she said with a sassy tone.

"Can you tell me why the threats were made?"

Lyric hesitated for a moment. Her green eyes flicked to me, then back to Paxton. "Probably because of something I'm investigating. I'm a journalist, after all."

"I suppose you're investigating Mia Sophia's death, right?"

Lyric made a hesitant nod of agreement.

Paxton frowned and shook his head. "Figures. That explains why you two are together."

"This was a professional hit," I said.

"What makes you say that?" Paxton asked.

"Somebody was smart enough to police up their brass. You're not going to find any shell casings."

"Maybe you took them?"

My face tensed, and my eyes blazed into him. "Besides checking the victim's vitals, I didn't touch anything."

"You compromised the crime scene."

I scowled at him.

"You should have called us when you saw signs of forced entry," Paxton said.

I gave him a sour look. "I didn't know what I'd find inside.

Someone could have been injured. I thought potentially saving a life would take precedence over crime scene integrity. Judging by the response times around here, I wasn't wrong to enter."

"You didn't save anybody," Paxton quipped. "It's a big city. It's not like the little town where you come from."

A crowd of neighbors had gathered around. Not many, but a few had seen the flashing lights and stepped into the streets in their PJs and robes to see what was going on.

A uniformed officer stepped to Paxton and muttered in his ear. A look of surprise washed over Paxton's face. Then his expression turned grim.

The officer left and stepped back inside.

"Your friend was a biochemist," Paxton said. "She worked at *Advanced DNA Analysis, LTD*."

Lyric nodded.

"The same lab that processed the toxicology report for Mia Sophia."

Lyric gave another hesitant nod.

"A call just went out over dispatch. Somebody torched it. Fire department is trying to contain the blaze now."

"Still think Mia Sophia's death was an *accidental drowning?*" I asked smugly.

30

"You don't think it's odd that a third-party lab has a discrepancy between their findings and the official autopsy report of the medical examiner? And the only person who can verify that discrepancy is dead, and the lab, and all the records, have been mysteriously set ablaze?" I asked.

Paxton grimaced. "Okay. I admit. Maybe there's something there."

He wasn't pleased about having to admit there was something screwy going on. And even less pleased it was pointed out to him by a reporter and an out-of-state sheriff's deputy.

A heavy breath escaped his nostrils. "Okay. Tell me everything you know."

I gave him the short version of everything I had discovered so far.

"That sounds crazy and far-fetched." He hesitated. "But not out of the realm of possibility," Paxton said.

I was surprised by his admission.

He motioned for us to step aside, we moved away from the entrance of the home and stepped down the walkway to his car.

In a hushed tone, he said, "I probably shouldn't be telling you this... Desmond Ross has had numerous complaints against him over the years. They've all gone away. All the girls signed non-disclosure agreements. The official investigations were dropped. No charges were ever filed. I've been trying to bust that guy for years. If what you're saying is true, this is a whole new level."

"I don't have anything concrete," I said. "But Desmond is the best lead I've got."

"I appreciate what you're doing," Paxton said. "But let me take it from here. I don't want to be standing over either of your corpses because you kept pushing on this thing." Paxton looked at me. "I know you can handle yourself. But I can assure you, the LAPD is on this." His eyes fell on Lyric. "Now go home, get some rest, and I will make sure there are extra patrols in your area for the next few days to keep an eye on things." He looked back at me. "You'll be the first to know if anything turns up. I promise."

We shook hands and strolled to the Ferrari. I slipped into the passenger seat, and Lyric cranked up the V12 and pulled away from the scene.

"I can't believe she's dead," Lyric said, still frazzled by the experience. "Do you think Desmond Ross is really capable of this?"

"I think Desmond Ross is capable of paying someone to do

it. It's doubtful he has the ability to do it himself. Guys like that never get their hands dirty."

We zipped through the canyon, over the hill, back to Lyric's house. We pulled into the driveway, and she killed the engine. I hopped out of the car and surveyed the area, then we cautiously pushed inside. Lyric deactivated the alarm, and I did another perimeter check for good measure.

The sun would be up soon, and both of us were pretty beat.

Lyric took my hand and led me up to her bedroom. "This has been such a stressful night. I need something pleasurable to take my mind off of things."

Despite my exhaustion, I still had enough energy to have a little fun.

31

I t seemed like I had just gotten to sleep when Lyric's alarm blasted. I was so tired at first, I didn't know what the hell was going on.

She killed the alarm and forced herself awake. She rolled over and kissed me on the cheek. "The news never sleeps. Gotta run. You can stay, or I can drop you at the hotel on my way to work."

I didn't have to think long about it. "I'll stay here."

"Make yourself at home. Lock up when you leave. Set the alarm. The code is 2112, in case, for some reason, you need it."

She gave me another peck on the cheek, then hopped out of bed and darted into the bathroom.

I rolled over and put the pillow over my head, falling back asleep. I heard her take a shower and get dressed, and the sound of the hairdryer was like torture. All things considered, she was out of the house pretty fast.

I heard the V12 crank up, and the exhaust note dissipated as she drove through the canyon.

It was a little before noon when I finally pulled myself out of bed. I hit the bathroom, took a shower, toweled off, then stumbled into the kitchen and fixed breakfast. After I tidied up, I caught a cab back to the hotel.

JD's band had arrived.

Dizzy and Crash were sprawled out on the couch, and Styxx was on the balcony, shouting at girls sunning themselves by the pool.

The band looked like hell and smelled even worse.

The drive from Coconut Key to Los Angeles was 43 hours. 2907 miles. They'd driven straight through, taking turns at the helm. Personally, I didn't think the shitty band van was capable of the journey. But somehow, they made it. It wouldn't take much recuperation for them to be ready to party.

"What happened to you?" JD asked.

"Long story," I said.

I filled him in on the details.

"No shit, huh? You really think the person that killed Mia is behind the biochemist?"

"Could be a random coincidence, but I doubt it." I sighed. "The fact that the lab was torched points to someone wanting to hide something."

"We can always kidnap Desmond Ross, put some persuasive

tactics to work, get him to fess up," JD said with a devious glint in his eyes.

I gave Jack a sideways glance. "I've been told to back off and let the LAPD handle this."

Jack's face crinkled. "When have you ever done what you're told?"

"I've got nothing to connect Desmond to this case whatsoever. Other than rumor, hearsay, and speculation."

"Maybe you ought to let the LAPD handle this one? Seems like it's getting a lot more complicated than originally anticipated."

"I told Mia's mother I'd get to the bottom of this. I promised. You know me. I keep my promises."

"What about Nikki Griffin?" JD asked. "I feel like she knows something she's not saying."

"Me too. I'm gonna work on her."

"Well, while you're working on that, I gotta hustle tickets to the show. As soon as these idiots recharge their batteries, we're gonna hit the strip and start pushing ticket sales."

"How are you going to do that?" I asked.

"I've got a plan," JD said with a sly grin.

32

There was a knock at the door. I pulled it open, and Scarlett stood there looking like the movie star that she was destined to become. She was still rocking the blonde hair, and in typical Hollywood fashion, she wore dark shades.

A shrill shriek of joy escaped her plump lips. She flung her arms around me, squeezing tight. "Oh, my God! Tyson. It's so great to see you!"

"Good to see you too!"

"What about me?" JD hollered.

"Ugh," Scarlett groaned. "You're so needy," she said, teasing him.

"I'm needy? I'll remember that next time you ask me to put money in your bank account."

Scarlett broke free of her embrace with me and strutted down the foyer to greet Jack in the living room. "You won't need to put money in my bank account much longer."

Scarlett was guaranteed a big payday when the Bree Taylor project went into production.

She gave Jack a hug that he gratefully accepted.

Dizzy and Crash perked up. Their eyes were about to pop out of their sockets, and their tongues hit the floor. They were practically drooling on themselves. Styxx took note from the balcony and hung in the archway, staring.

Scarlett was drool-worthy.

"Who's this?" Dizzy asked.

Jack scowled at his bandmates. "This is my daughter. And she's off-limits."

Scarlett smiled. "She introduced herself to the band and shook their hands.

"Pleasure to make your acquaintance," Crash said, bowing as if Scarlett were royalty.

Styxx ventured in from the balcony and greeted her as well. "I'm the drummer."

"That means he's the mentally challenged one," Dizzy said.

Styxx smacked him playfully. "Don't mind him. He plucks things for a living."

"I'm the foundation," Crash said. "I lay down the groove and hold the whole thing together. They'd be hollow without me."

"I've been hearing lots of stories," Scarlett said. "I'm looking forward to the show. You better not disappoint."

"Don't worry. We won't disappoint," Dizzy assured.

"How was Vegas?" I asked.

Scarlett smiled "I left with more money than I went with. I call that a good day."

"Aren't you a little too young to be gambling?" Jack asked, attempting to exercise some of his parental authority.

"It's not my fault that nobody carded me."

Scarlett sniffled and wiped her nose. That instantly triggered Jack's alarm. He leaned in, eyeing her suspiciously. "Pull off the shades, let me see your eyes."

Scarlett's face crinkled. "What's wrong with you?"

"Take off the sunglasses," JD commanded.

She huffed but complied. She opened her eyes exaggeratedly and stared back at JD. "I'm not high. It's more than I can say for some people in this room."

Ever since the band arrived, the suite reeked of marijuana.

"Have a little faith, Jack," Scarlett said.

"I just don't want to see you falling off the wagon," JD said.

"Not even a consideration," Scarlett assured. "Relax."

She'd had her battles in the past with multiple substances, but had been keeping her nose clean.

Jack surveyed her closely for another moment, then conceded that she was probably clean. She didn't look tweaked out to me.

The guys in the band continued to ogle Scarlett.

"You're not jailbait, are you?" Dizzy asked.

Scarlett chuckled. "You're safe. I'm legal."

Dizzy breathed a sigh of relief. "Good to know. I was starting to worry, thinking I might be a pervert for getting a chub."

Scarlett laughed.

JD scowled at him.

"You're a pervert, all right," Styxx said. "Don't worry."

"Blow me," Dizzy said.

"Sorry, you're not my type," Styxx replied.

"Did I fail to mention that this is my daughter?" JD asked.

"Well, your daughter is hot," Crash said.

Scarlett giggled.

"We need to put her on our album cover," Dizzy said. "That would be rad."

Scarlett shrugged. "I'm down."

"We are not objectifying my daughter on our album cover."

"It's not objectification," Dizzy assured. "It's a celebration of female beauty."

"I don't think a girl chained to a stack of amplifiers, wearing nothing but a dog collar is a celebration."

"Slave to rock 'n' roll, dude!" Dizzy said. "It's the perfect album title."

"Thrash says you're an actress," Crash said.

Scarlett arched a curious eyebrow. "Thrash?"

"My stage name," JD said, flatly.

Scarlett giggled again.

"Would you have been in anything we might have seen?" Crash continued.

"Well, you'll get to see me in the upcoming Bree Taylor project, thanks to Tyson."

"No shit? That's big time!"

Scarlett smiled.

Crash pulled out his phone and started searching the Internet. A moment later, he asked, "So, do you go by Scarlett Nicole?"

She nodded.

He searched again.

His eyes went wide. He zoomed in to get a better look at the images he'd found.

Scarlett's eyes narrowed at him. "Are you looking at my tits?"

"No," Crash said, innocently. He swallowed hard, then looked at his phone again. "That's you?"

"From a horror movie that... well, long story."

Jack scowled at Crash.

He shrugged. "What? I'm just looking her up on the Internet."

"Well, stop."

"Nice tits, though," Crash said.

"Thank you," Scarlett replied proudly.

"I mean, very classy."

Jack's eyes were on fire. He snatched the phone from Crash's hand. "Don't you idiots have something better to do?"

"We've been in a car for 43 hours. I am not doing shit but lounging around and getting high."

"We've got tickets to sell," JD reminded them. "We're here for a reason."

"Oh yeah, right," Crash said.

"Well, I guess I'll leave you to your ticket sales," Scarlett said.

She gave JD a hug.

Jack looked disappointed. "You're leaving so soon?"

"Yeah. I told Audrey I'd meet her for a late lunch."

"You haven't seen your old man in ages, and he treks halfway across the country to see you, and you can't spend an afternoon with him?"

"Needy," Scarlett teased.

Jack's face soured.

"And you didn't trek halfway across the country just to see me. You came to play a show at *Sour Mash*."

"Well, seeing you certainly factored into my decision."

"Why don't we have dinner sometime this week? You can take me to a fancy Beverly Hills restaurant, and I can point out all the celebrities."

"I'm gonna hold you to it," JD said.

"You know I'm not going to pass up a free meal at a fancy restaurant."

"We get to go too, right?" Crash asked.

JD frowned at him.

Scarlett smiled, hugged JD again, and kissed him on the cheek.

She waved to the band as she started toward the door. "Nice to meet you, boys."

They all checked out her ass as she strode away.

JD shot them dirty looks.

Scarlett gave me a hug and a kiss on the cheek and said she'd be in touch.

I pulled open the door, and she stepped into the hallway, put on her shades, and wiggled her fingers goodbye.

I pushed the door shut and turned back to the room.

"So, dude, how did you produce that?" Dizzy asked JD.

Jack's face was red. "I just want to take this opportunity to remind each and every one of you, I have a gun, and I will use it."

33

J D had hired a mobile billboard to roll up and down the Sunset Strip with the image of the band in full '80s regalia. The massive image featured the band with lots of flowing hair, and JD blowing a kiss into the camera. The *Wild Fury* logo was prominently displayed as well as the dates of the show at *Sour Mash*. Speakers blasted *Wild Fury* originals as the truck towed the mobile billboard down the boulevard.

Jack and company hit the sidewalks, selling tickets, handing out flyers, causing a ruckus. He'd hired two porn stars from the agency to accompany them. The girls wore bikinis, prancing around in stiletto heels, shaking their wares.

The event caused quite a stir, even in Hollywood.

I tagged along and offered moral support, passing out flyers and helping as much as I could. Cars honked, and passersby hollered. Even in West Hollywood, the girls drew attention.

Afterward, we returned to the hotel bar for happy hour. Marcel was working and served us a round of drinks.

JD and the band were excited. They had a good day. They sold a bunch of tickets, created awareness, and even got interviewed by a local news station. JD had some radio interviews set up at a few local stations as well.

I texted Lyric to see how her day was going and if she was safe.

I didn't hear back right away.

Marcel leaned against the counter and quietly muttered, "You know, I've been thinking about it. That night, I remember Mia meeting with someone else after Desmond."

I lifted an intrigued eyebrow. "Really?"

Marcel looked around, cautiously. "Yeah. Some guy. I wouldn't call him a regular, but I think I've seen him in here before."

"What did he look like?"

Marcel shrugged. "I really can't say. It was dark."

"Start with the basics. Short, tall, thin, fat?"

"Average guy. Little on the short side. Leather jacket, brown hair, mustache. Had a scar across his right eye."

I knew instantly who he was talking about. "Are you sure?"

"I think."

Eyewitness testimony was notoriously inaccurate.

I pulled out my phone and launched a photos app, showing Marcel a picture of Chuck Paxton.

"That's him. That's the guy."

"You sure?"

"Positive."

I told JD, and his face crinkled with suspicion. "Why the hell would Paxton be meeting with Mia Sophia on the night of her death?"

The wheels turned, and it didn't take long for all the pieces to fit together. "Amber Angel said Mia was busted. But there was no record of an arrest. What if Paxton was the arresting officer?"

JD's brow lifted, intrigued.

"What if he was blackmailing her? Mia would have done anything to keep that information from reaching the public. Up-and-coming star... Her career about to take off... The last thing she needed was to be outed as a former prostitute."

JD pondered the information. "That would explain a lot of things." He paused. "What do we do now?"

"We find a way to connect the dots."

I texted Nikki Griffin and laid it all out. [I know about Chuck Paxton. I think he may have been involved in Mia Sophia's death. I think he was blackmailing her. I think he's probably been blackmailing you for years.]

It was a risky move.

If she *did* have a relationship with Paxton, as I surmised, she may go straight to him. Paxton wasn't necessarily a guy I wanted to get on the wrong side of. Not just yet. Not before I had more ammunition.

I waited for a reply.

34

I t was an hour later when I received a text from an unknown number. *[Meet me at Marina del Rey at II PM.]*

[Who is this?]

[Someone you want to talk to. Meet me in the parking lot of Basin K off Tonga Way.]

[I'm not a big fan of walking into unknown situations.]

[I'm taking a big risk just by talking to you.]

[How did you get my number?]

[Mutual acquaintance. II PM. Come alone.]

I texted Isabella and asked her to locate the phone where the text originated. She replied a few minutes later. *[Burner phone in Marina del Rey.]*

My curiosity was piqued.

My gut told me this was a contact of Nikki Griffin's. That could be a good thing or a bad thing. I wasn't sure which.

I looked at my watch. It was 7 PM.

We left the bar, and the band staggered into the restaurant. They needed a good meal after 43 hours on the road, eating fast food and gas station snacks. JD picked up the tab, and we all feasted like kings.

After dinner, the band was ready to hit the strip and party like rockstars. JD was determined to keep up with the youngsters. I had no doubt that the rest of the evening would descend into a drunk and debaucherous affair.

I didn't tell Jack about my clandestine meeting with the anonymous individual. He would have insisted that he accompany me, but I didn't want to ruin his fun. He was having a good time with the band living out his rock 'n' roll fantasy. I figured I could handle it alone. I just needed to be smart about it.

I had heard back from Lyric, and she invited me up to the hills. She didn't want to be alone, and I couldn't blame her. I told Jack I'd catch up with him later.

"How many days in a row have you seen this girl?"

I coughed, "Three."

He shook his head. "And you got on me about *one-itis?* This is beginning to sound serious."

"It's not serious. After what happened last night, she just wants somebody around."

"Serious," he teased.

"Shut up."

"I think you might need to see a doctor about this condition."

I chuckled. "You're one to talk. All I hear is *Sloan this... Sloan that...*"

"Have I said one word about her tonight?"

"No, but I'm sure you'll be texting her all evening."

"Don't worry. I'm playing it cool. Just a few texts here and there to let her know I'm interested. Not too much, not too little."

I rolled my eyes.

We all headed back up to the room for a minute. JD and the crew formulated their plan of attack for the evening, deciding on the clubs they wanted to hit. I press-checked my weapon, then called for a Zoomber.

I wished the guys well in their evening adventure, then headed down to the lobby.

The Zoomber spun me up to the hills and dropped me off curbside at Lyric's home. I stepped onto the sidewalk, scanned the area, then strolled up the driveway to the porch. I kept my head on a swivel, not taking any chances.

I rang the bell, and a moment later, Lyric pulled open the door with an inviting smile. She gave me a hug as I stepped into the foyer. "I'm glad you're here."

"I can't stay long. I need to get down to Marina del Rey."

"What for?"

I caught her up to speed.

"I'm going with you," she insisted.

I shook my head. "No. You're not. I have no idea what I'm stepping into."

I reached down and pulled a subcompact Bösch-Haüer PPQ-X5 9mm that was holstered around my ankle. It was a smaller version of my favorite X2. I press-checked the weapon and made sure it was on safety. "Have you ever shot a gun before?"

She shook her head.

I gave her an overview of the basic operation. Then handed the weapon to her.

"What am I supposed to do with this?"

"Just in case of emergency."

She looked terrified—both by the pistol and by the situation.

"You're telling me a dirty cop may be responsible for Mia Sophia's death, along with Sidney's... and you think a gun is gonna help me feel safe?"

"Safer."

"I need to talk to my segment producer. We need to go public with this."

"We have no hard evidence linking Paxton to anything yet. A vague confirmation from a bartender that the two met is not enough."

I paused. "Why don't you check into the Château under an assumed name? You should be safer there."

She thought for a moment, then agreed. "I'll get my things together."

"Turn your cell phone off."

"What? Why?"

"In case someone is tracking your location. You need to lay low until I get this situation sorted."

"How are you going to get the situation sorted? Do you have any idea what you're up against? If Paxton is involved in this, we don't know how deep his network goes."

"Better yet. Leave your phone on, and leave it here. If anyone is tracking you, it might throw them off."

She packed a small bag and set the alarm before leaving. She handed me the keys to the Ferrari. "You drive. You can take it down to Marina del Rey."

"That's trusting of you. You've never seen me drive."

"Something tells me you're competent."

She threw her bag in the trunk and hopped into the passenger seat. I cranked up the engine, and the exhaust rumbled.

Lyric cautioned me to go easy out of the driveway. I angled the nose of the car to avoid scraping, then cruised out of the neighborhood.

I took a convoluted route back to the Château, making sure I wasn't tailed. When I was sure it was safe, I pulled into the hotel.

Lyric gave me a kiss on the cheek before hopping out of the car. "Be safe."

"You too."

"Call me after your meeting. And don't trash my car."

35

I doubled back a few times, looped around, and took an unconventional route. I was pretty sure I hadn't been followed to the marina.

The parking lot was sparse. Boats swayed in the slips, and lights glistened off the inky water. I stayed in the car for a moment, surveying the area. I didn't see anyone around.

I finally pushed open the door, stepped out of the vehicle, and ambled toward the dock, my eyes peering deep into the shadows. There was an office building in the center of the parking lot, and two dumpsters to the side along with a storage shed. I carefully wandered around them, heading toward the water. A voice from deep in the shadows, behind the storage shed, hissed, "Deputy Wild?"

I palmed my pistol, keeping it in its holster. A beautiful blonde emerged from the darkness. She glanced around cautiously before stepping into the light. "Were you followed?"

"No. I took precautions."

The sickly green glow of an overhead mercury vapor light illuminated her face and sparkled her eyes. She scanned the parking lot nervously. When she was satisfied, she said, "Follow me."

She led me to the dock, and we walked past slips of speed-boats, motor yachts, and sailboats. We reached a 25-meter *Marchetti*. Across the garage, written in elegant script, the name *Nauti-Gal* was painted in gold-flake metallic.

It was a nice boat. Elegant lines that looked like they were carved by the wind. A boarding gate to starboard allowed the blonde to step to the aft deck. There was an alfresco dining area with a stone tabletop, rimmed in teak, surrounded by U-shaped all-weather seating. Stairs led down to the hydraulic swim platform which held a 7-foot tender. A molded-in stairway led from the aft deck to the flybridge above.

The blonde slid open the glass door to the salon and disappeared inside.

I hesitated on the dock, glanced around again, not sure what I was stepping into.

She poked her head through the hatch and hissed, "Hurry."

I climbed aboard, then advanced to the salon, keeping a ready hand on my pistol. My eyes surveyed the areas for threats.

The salon was open and airy. Large windows allowed a panoramic view of the marina. They were tinted, and from the outside it was impossible to see in unless a light was on inside.

There was plenty of modern, comfortable seating with contrasting joinery. Forward of the salon was the helm. A forward stairwell led below deck to the guest quarters.

There could have been anyone below deck. It left an unsettled feeling in my gut.

The blonde slid the hatch shut after I stepped into the salon.

"Is this your boat?"

She shook her head. "No. It's a friend's."

"Which friend?"

She hesitated a moment. "Nikki. She says you might be able to help."

I kept a wary eye on the forward stairs. "Is anyone else aboard?"

"No."

"Mind if I check?"

"Knock yourself out."

I edged forward and drew my weapon. I crept down the steps and scanned the companionway.

It was clear.

Forward, the VIP guest suite was equipped with a queen berth and private en suite. I carefully pushed inside and cleared the area. There was another guest quarters amidships, and a full-beam master aft. This was a damn nice boat, elegantly appointed with soft, comfortable spaces with clean lines, and a light, airy feeling.

I searched all the compartments, then returned to the salon.

The blonde waited nervously, chewing her fingernails.

"Okay, what's going on?"

"Nikki says you might be able to do something about Chuck Paxton?"

"What can you tell me about him? And what was his relationship with Mia?"

She took a deep breath. Her frazzled brown eyes gazed at me with a mix of caution mixed with hopefulness. "It started a few years ago when I was working for Nikki."

"You don't work for her any longer?"

"Not on a regular basis. Only when things get really tight. This is going to sound weird, but Nikki has really been there for me whenever I needed her. She let me come and go as I pleased, never gave me any grief for wanting to quit the business. She's been really good to a lot of the girls, helping them get on their feet, helping them get out of the business if they want to."

"Let me guess... You were with Mia when Chuck Paxton busted both of you."

Her eyes widened. "How did you know?"

"Because all the pieces add up."

"He said he wouldn't arrest us if we did, you know, favors for him. At the time, I thought, great... keeps an arrest off my record. Just the cost of doing business. But the favors never stopped. Even when I got out of the business. Paxton demanded I still perform, you know, *services*, for him at his leisure or he'd expose me. I just started dating a new guy. Everything's going great. I don't want him to ever know about my former life. I feel terrible because I have to go and do *things* with that horrible man whenever he calls."

I cringed, disgusted by what I heard. Paxton was a scumbag.

"He did the same thing to Mia," she continued.

"She was about to turn the tables on him."

"You two still kept in touch?" I asked, surprised.

"Yeah. We had bonded in this weird way. We didn't talk a lot, but when we did, it was just like the old days. I think I was the only one she could talk to about this stuff. She said she was finally going to get us out from under Paxton's thumb."

"How so?"

"Every time we had sex with Paxton, he filmed it and took pictures. It was an ever-growing arsenal of material to use against us. But two can play that game. Mia began recording all of their interactions. Every time he demanded sex. Every time he threatened her. I guess she had gained enough success that she felt like she could go public. I think the current climate encouraged her. She stopped fearing repercussions."

"So Paxton killed her?"

"I don't have proof. But there's no doubt in my mind. Mia had a coke habit..."

"I know."

"Paxton would always give us a little to sweeten the deal. It didn't cost him anything. He got it off the street from a bust or one of his informants."

"I have a witness that places him at the hotel bar the night of her death. Do you think he could have given her cocaine laced with fentanyl that night?"

The blonde nodded. "That would have been easy for him."

"Are you willing to testify against him?"

Her terrified eyes filled with dread. "I don't know. I mean, I'd never make it to trial. You see what Paxton and his crew are capable of. He's been harassing and blackmailing Nikki for years. She wants him gone as much as anybody else. I'm kind of surprised Nikki hasn't hired someone to do it."

"Why do you think she hasn't?"

"That's not in her nature. Nikki's got a good heart."

"How many dirty cops does Paxton work with?"

The blonde shrugged. "I don't know. But you see how dangerous it is to get on Paxton's bad side." She paused. "Is there anything you can do? I mean, you're a cop. But Nikki says you're not local."

"Not local. I have no jurisdiction here."

She deflated. "Then you can't do anything."

"If I can gather enough evidence, I can take it to the District Attorney or the Office of the Inspector General."

"You can't take it to internal affairs. They'll dismiss the whole thing. Paxton has friends, connections. You know how much money these guys make extorting people? Nobody wants that gravy train to end."

"I'll bring him down. I don't know how, but I will. You have to give me your word you will testify. Otherwise, I've got nothing."

"How can you keep me safe?" she asked, incredulous.

36

"You never told me your name," I said.

The blonde hesitated. "I don't know if I want to tell you my name."

"I can't help you if you're not going to trust me."

"Sorry, but trust is not something that comes easy for me."

"That makes two of us."

She was silent for a long moment. "Bonnie."

"Nice to meet you, Bonnie."

She smiled, and we shook hands.

"Who knows you're here?" I asked.

"Nikki and the guy I'm dating," Bonnie said.

"How long have you been dating?"

"A few weeks. Why?"

I hesitated. "No reason." I paused. "The phone you called me from..."

"It's a prepaid cellular. My ex-boyfriend is a psychopath. I got a disposable phone because he was stalking me. I think he put software to track me on my old phone."

"Sounds like a nice guy," I said with more than a trace of sarcasm.

"Sometimes, I think my picker is broken. But I swear, the guy I am dating now is really nice. At least he seems that way."

"Don't tell anyone what we discussed."

"What about Nikki?"

"Do you trust her?"

"She's the only reason I'm talking to you. She's always been there for me. Yes, I trust her."

Before leaving the salon, I promised her I would do everything I could to bring Chuck Paxton down.

I slid open the glass door and stepped to the aft deck. My wary eyes surveyed the marina. At this time of night, there wasn't much activity. A few lights were on from liveaboards, but not much traffic about the dock.

I passed through the boarding gate and stepped to the dock. Waves lapped against hulls and riggings clanked against masts as I strolled back to the parking lot.

I chirped the alarm to the Ferrari, and the lights flashed. My eyes kept scanning the shadows of the empty lot. When I reached the car, I pulled open the door, slid behind the wheel, and pulled the door shut with a thunk. I cranked up the massive engine, and the throaty exhaust growled. This thing was anything but inconspicuous. But it was damn fun to drive. It was the kind of car where driving 100 MPH felt like 35 MPH.

I eased out of the parking lot and made my way back to the 405 freeway, which would take me north toward West Los Angeles.

Before I knew it, I was flying down the freeway at triple digits. Running through the gears with the paddle shifter was a lot of fun. When I realized how fast I was going, my foot backed off the gas, and I let the Italian beast coast to a reasonable speed.

I took a right on the 10 freeway, then exited La Cienega heading north toward West Hollywood and the Sunset Strip.

The light at the intersection ahead changed from green to yellow. It was in that in-between stage, and my foot let off the gas slightly. Then I changed my mind and floored it.

It was a stupid thing to do.

If you want my honest opinion, I was in the intersection when the light changed from yellow to red. Perfectly legal. But I don't think the LAPD officer who pulled up behind me, flashing his red and blues, saw it the same way.

The siren howled, and a jolt of energy traveled down my spine, standing the hairs on my neck tall. My stomach twisted. Nobody likes to see flashing lights behind them, not even a cop.

I pulled to the curb by the parking meters just past West Olympic.

This was a bad scenario.

The officer sat in his vehicle for a moment, running the plates.

I rolled down the driver's side window and stuck my hands out in plain view, holding my shiny gold badge.

It took a few moments for the door of the patrol car to swing open. The officer stepped out and started toward me, the beam of a Mag-lite flashlight spotting me.

"Evening, officer," I said with a smile, trying to diffuse the situation.

"Sir, I pulled you over because you ran the red light."

"My apologies. I could have sworn it was yellow when I entered the intersection. Won't happen again."

"Sir, are you carrying?"

"I am. Our department requires it."

Maybe he didn't like the fact that I flashed my get out of jail free card. He proceeded with the stop.

"I'm going to need you to step out of the vehicle carefully. Keep your hands where I can see them."

He took a step back, keeping one hand on his pistol and the other hand aiming the beam of the flashlight in my eyes.

Cars blew past us on La Cienega.

I pushed open the door and emerged from the vehicle with my hands in the air, still clutching onto my badge.

"I need you to step around to the rear of the vehicle," the officer commanded.

"Sure thing." I complied with his request.

With my hands in the air and my jacket gaping open, it was easy to see my pistol in its Kydex holster perched in my waistband.

The officer drew his pistol and aimed it at me.

I didn't like where this was going. I didn't like it at all.

"You see that I'm a fellow police officer?" I asked.

"I do, sir."

That fact didn't seem to change his demeanor.

My face tightened.

"With your thumb and index finger, I need you to remove the weapon and set it on the ground in front of you."

This was the part I didn't like. All kinds of scenarios flashed through my mind. He could easily say I was going for my pistol, then discharge his weapon in self-defense.

"How about you write me a ticket for running the red light, and we call it a night?"

"Are you failing to comply with my request?"

What an asshole.

37

"I'm sorry, but I'm not exactly comfortable reaching for my weapon while you have your pistol aimed at me," I said. "I feel like you're on edge. A little twitchy. You can see how that creates a problem for me."

"It's going to create a bigger problem if you don't comply," the officer barked.

"Toss me the handcuffs. I'll put them on, and you can take my pistol yourself. That's a fair trade, isn't it?"

He put the flashlight under his armpit, still keeping the beam aimed at me along with his pistol. He pulled the cuffs from a pouch on his utility belt and tossed them to me. I slapped them on my wrists behind my back.

The officer inched forward and removed my pistol from the holster.

He took a step back, commanded me to stay put, and returned to his patrol car. He set my weapon somewhere inside. The headlights made it difficult to see inside the vehicle.

Was this guy a rookie with an attitude? Or did he happen to be friends with Detective Paxton?

Cars continued to buzz by, swirling gusts of wind around me. Some of them honked, while others shouted, feeling elated that they weren't in my shoes.

"Have you had anything to drink tonight?" the officer asked when he returned.

"Yeah, I had a few drinks six hours ago."

"How many is a few?"

"Two. I had two drinks with dinner six hours ago. Is this always how you treat visiting law enforcement?"

"Sir, when I was near your person, I smelled a significant odor of alcoholic beverage. I'm going to need to initiate a field sobriety exam."

"Seriously?"

"I believe you to be intoxicated."

Anger swelled within, but I managed to contain myself. "At this point, I'm going to respectfully decline any testing you may offer."

"So, you're refusing to comply?"

"Yes."

"Have it your way. I'm placing you under arrest. You have the right to remain silent..."

At this point, I knew to shut the hell up. There was no

talking my way out of anything. He escorted me to the patrol car and stuffed me in the backseat.

Officer Dickweed climbed behind the wheel, put the car into gear, and drove away from the scene.

"What about the vehicle?" I asked.

"It will be impounded."

He didn't call dispatch. He didn't arrange for a tow truck. He didn't let anyone know he had a suspect in custody.

That's when I started to grow concerned. I wondered if he had even called in the stop.

"I suppose you know Detective Paxton?" I asked.

The officer's eyes flicked to me in the rearview mirror. It was all the confirmation I needed. He knew Paxton, alright. I could see it in his eyes.

We headed downtown, well past any substation. I knew I was screwed. We cruised down Wilshire for a while. Things got doubly concerning when he turned down a dark alley.

He parked the car by the dumpster. Before he climbed out of the vehicle, I asked, "Is this where you take all the drunk drivers?"

He slammed the door, moved to the rear door, and yanked it open. "Get out!"

I slid across the seat, and he grabbed my arm, pulling me out of the vehicle. Another car pulled into the alleyway, blocking the exit, the high-beam headlights squinting my eyes.

The oncoming car stopped, and two men exited. I couldn't

make them out through the glare of the headlights until they stepped around the front of the vehicle. It was Detective Paxton and another man.

Not surprising.

"He's all yours," Officer Dickweed said.

"Thanks. We'll handle it from here."

With a smug tone, the officer said, "Have a nice evening."

I wondered how much he knew about Paxton. Did he know what a scumbag he was?

He climbed back into his patrol car and sped away down the alley, the smell of exhaust filling my nostrils. It smelled rich, like the O2 sensor was going bad.

A streetlight on Wilshire cast long shadows in the alley. Scraps of newspaper scraped against the concrete. The passageway smelled like body odor and urine. There were trash bags lined against the wall, and cardboard boxes had been flattened into makeshift mattresses. Though, there didn't appear to be any current homeless residents occupying the alleyway at the moment.

Paxton had an annoyed, but smug look on his face. He had the upper hand, and he was going to make sure I knew it. "You've become a real pain in my ass."

"Is this the part where you beat me to a pulp, tell me to get out of town, and never come back?"

He chuckled. "I'm a civilized man. I would never do anything like that."

"No. Of course not. You'd have somebody else do it for you."

He smiled. "I gotta hand it to you. Nothing gets past you, does it?"

"No. It doesn't."

"Come on, smart ass," he said, grabbing my arm. "Your time is up."

He dragged me to his car and stuffed me in the back. Then he and his partner climbed in up front. Paxton backed out of the alley and continued toward east LA. He wasn't taking me to the station. That much was certain.

38

East of downtown, the sidewalks of 5th Street were lined with tents and makeshift lean-tos built from tarps. Trash cluttered the area, and graffiti tagged the walls.

We cruised deeper through the urban chaos, heading toward the LA River. The wide, concrete channel that cut through the center of the city had been home to numerous action movie car chases over the years. The area under the 6th Street viaduct was an iconic part of Hollywood's movie history.

But the bridge was gone now.

Demolished because of the weakening structure. The nondescript tunnel off El Rey Street that led down to the river was blocked. The area was undergoing an urban renewal. A new bridge would be built. More coffee shops and markets would spring up. Warehouses would be reclaimed and turned into high-end housing. Property taxes would increase. But as it stood, it still wasn't an area you wanted to be after dark.

Paxton pulled the vehicle into an empty construction site near the railyard that ran along the river. The foundations of a building had been laid. There were several concrete pylons supporting four unfinished floors. There was lots of scaffolding and rebar. Construction debris brimmed from industrial dumpsters, and heavy equipment hibernated during off-hours.

Paxton's unmarked car crunched over the gravel of the construction yard and ground to a halt. Four thugs emerged from the shadows and stood in the beam of the headlights.

It didn't take a brain surgeon to figure out what was going on. Paxton would keep his hands clean. He'd have someone else do the dirty work for him.

Paxton stepped out of the car and approached the thugs. They exchanged a few words. I couldn't hear what they were saying.

Paxton's partner in the passenger seat said nothing. The big ogre had a short blonde buzz cut and a big chin. He was a broad-shouldered guy and looked like he could have been a boxer back in the day. I had no doubt he could take a punch or two or ten.

"Hey, Big Guy," I said. "What's your name?"

"What the fuck is it to you?"

"I just want to be able to put a name to a face when I kill you."

That got his attention. He craned his neck over his shoulder, and his blue eyes blazed into me. A smug smirk tugged his lips. "When you get to hell, tell 'em Duke sent you."

"I'm sure you'll be waiting when I get there."

Paxton moved back to the car, opened the rear door, and pulled me out of it. "I want to introduce you to your new friends."

He marched me around the front of the car, into the beam of the headlights. The thugs' narrow eyes surveyed me like wolves, ready to tear into flesh.

There were lots of gang tattoos, wife-beater T-shirts, and plaid work shirts. One of them gripped a lead pipe. I had no doubt I would get acquainted with it soon.

Paxton cocked his fist back and hammered a punch into my kidneys. My back buckled around his fist, and I dropped to my knees.

I gritted my teeth and stifled a groan.

Paxton knelt down, released the handcuffs from around my wrists, then kicked me in the back, shoving me to the ground.

My hands broke my fall, but I still got a face full of dirt. As I was starting to get up, a thug took the opportunity to kick me in the belly. The force of the impact rolled me onto my back.

Paxton lorded over me. "Enjoy the rest of your life, scum-bag." He chuckled. "All five minutes of it."

"I'd watch your back if I were you," I said, my jaw tight, trying to act like the boot to the gut was no big deal.

Paxton chuckled again. "You got heart, I'll give you that."

His footsteps crunched against the gravel as he moved back to the car and climbed into the vehicle. The door slammed shut, and the car clunked into gear. The heat from the engine and the ticking of the lifters faded away. So did the light from the headlight as the vehicle backed out of the construction site, the tires rolling over the gravel, crackling and popping.

The gang unleashed fury.

A torrent of boots found my rib cage. I was kicked and beaten from all angles. Plumes of dust rose around me from the dry gravel, filling the air with haze. With each breath, I inhaled more of the dry, powdery dust, causing me to choke.

Fists and boots pummeled my body. My lips were split. My cheeks lacerated. The metallic taste of blood filled my mouth, and I drooled a pinkish goo onto the dirt. The ping of the metal pipe rang out with every strike against my body. Pain rifled through me, searing and sharp.

There was nothing I could do.

I was sure this was the end.

My body would end up in a dumpster. Probably set on fire. Maybe I'd be tossed into the river or buried in a shallow grave.

I couldn't breathe. My lungs were on fire. My ribs were cracked.

I was on the verge of blacking out when a voice said, "Stop."

It was timid at first.

The beating continued.

"Stop!" the voice said with more force.

"Stop, I said!" the voice shouted.

The beating slowly dissipated.

I could barely move. My swollen eyes peered up at the blurry faces. One drew closer and hovered over me, examining my features.

"That's him!" the voice said. It belonged to a kid, maybe 14. The face came into focus, and I recognized the yellow jersey. Number eight from the liquor store robbery.

"That's the guy who saved Eduardo," the kid continued.

"You sure about that?" the leader of the gang asked. He wore a white T-shirt and khaki pants that were now spotted with my blood.

"That's him. I know it. He chased me. Eduardo would be dead if it weren't for him."

The gang leader gave me a hard look. Then he told the kid, "Look at him again. Are you sure?"

"Positive!"

The gang leader leaned over me with his hands on his knees. "Antonio says you saved my little brother. That true?"

I could barely choke out the words, "If your little brother is the kid that knocked off the liquor store on Sunset, then yeah. If not, I don't know what to tell you."

The gang leader hesitated for a moment, looking torn. "This puts me in a difficult position."

"Want to switch places?" I asked.

A slight chuckle escaped his lips. "See, around here, we take care of our own. You took care of my brother. I owe you a debt. But I also never break my word. And I promised Paxton I would take care of his problem."

"I'm just a guy looking for the truth."

"Looks like you found it." He paused. "The way I see it, you've got two choices. Me and my boys here can finish the job, and Paxton's problem goes away. Or, I let you go, and you disappear. You get out of town, forget about the truth, and Paxton is none the wiser."

"What's your angle with Paxton?"

"That's none of your business. Now, what's it going to be?"

"I think this is my cue to leave town," I said.

"Smart man." With a low, stern voice, he warned, "My debt to you is paid. If I ever see you again, or if you embarrass me by showing your face around town, I will find you and kill you. You got that?"

"I got it."

He stood up and signaled to his gang. They backed away and left the construction site. The lead pipe clinked as the thug tossed it on the ground near me. The kid knelt down and snatched my watch from my wrist. I was too worked over to care. Gravel crunched under the soles of their shoes as they disappeared.

I staggered to my feet. My head throbbed, my temples pounded, my back hurt, my arms were bruised and sore, more than one rib was cracked, and my thighs had a deep, aching pain.

Paxton had taken my cell phone, my wallet, and keys. I had nothing, and I was in a bad part of town.

Things were looking grim. I couldn't imagine how they could get worse, but clearly I wasn't using my imagination well enough.

39

Each step was an agonizing, monumental task. Zombies had better strides. I staggered north on El Rey Street. It wasn't long before a car passed by, an old Impala—white droptop with red interior. It circled the block and passed by again. This time two thugs hopped out, and I found myself on the business end of a pistol. The smell of gunpowder and oil filled my nostrils.

"Give me your fucking money!"

A faint chuckle escaped my swollen lips.

"What's so funny?"

"Do I look like I have a nickel to my name?"

The thug looked me up and down. "You look like shit, actually. What happened, your old lady get pissed at you?"

I chuckled again, and it hurt like hell.

"Empty your pockets!" the thug commanded.

I turned them out—there was nothing but lint.

"No watch? Nothing?"

I held my wrist and dangled it, displaying the fact it was bare.

The thug shook his head. "Waste my time. I ought to shoot you on principle."

"Go ahead," I stared at him flatly, not giving a shit.

He snorted and dismissively waved his hand at me before he climbed back into the car. The goons sped away, and the tires squealed as they rounded the corner.

I kept heading north, under the 4th Street bridge. I quickly found myself in a revitalized area. Renovated warehouses and newly built condominiums. All the stores were closed, but there were juice bars, health food stores, and yoga studios. It wouldn't be long before the whole area was as tame as the suburbs.

I stumbled into the parking lot of a strip-mall, looking for a payphone. My knee buckled, and I tripped and fell. I smacked the concrete, and another jolt of pain shot through my body. I couldn't move. I just lay there. My body throbbed, and my head was fuzzy.

I could have been there for a minute or twenty. I wasn't sure. I may have passed out for a moment.

"Hey, Mister, are you okay?" a woman asked, hovering over me.

I could barely see out the slits that were my eyes. Her face was fuzzy.

"Just peachy," I replied.

"You need to get to a hospital," she said.

"No hospitals."

"I'm calling 911."

"No. I'm fine."

"You don't look fine."

I tried to sit up. The world spun.

"What happened? Did you get mugged?"

I nodded. "Something like that."

"Oh my God, that's terrible! I thought this neighborhood was getting safer." She paused. "You really shouldn't be out wandering around after dark."

"Why aren't you following your own advice?"

"Because I was out for a jog. And I know where to go and where not to go. I run pretty fast."

She wore yoga pants and a sports bra. Judging by how flat her stomach was, I figured she spent a lot of time crafting her physique. It was a good one. She had short dark hair, alluring brown eyes, and beautiful bone structure. For a moment, I thought I was dreaming.

She helped me to my feet.

The ground swayed as I stood, like I was aboard a ship. She held me steady.

She looked to be about college-age.

"Are you sure you don't want me to call the cops or something?

"No cops!" I barked.

"Why no cops?" Her suspicious eyes surveyed me.

"I'm a deputy sheriff."

"Oh." Her face twisted with confusion.

"Undercover," I added.

"Where's your badge?" she asked, still skeptical.

"With my gun, my wallet, and my cell phone." I sighed. "If you need to verify my identity, you can contact Sheriff Wayne Daniels with the Coconut County Sheriff's Department."

"Coconut County?" Her face scrunched up. "What are you doing here?"

"It's a long story. Let's just say I got a little too close to uncovering something that powerful people didn't want uncovered."

I took a step and teetered, then almost tumbled back down. The girl caught me before I fell.

Her face tensed, and she looked me up and down. I could tell she was conflicted. "You really are in bad shape," she said. "I don't usually do this, but you look pretty harmless—especially in your condition. If you're not going to go to the hospital, at least come back to my apartment, get cleaned up, and rest for a bit."

I accepted her generosity, and she helped me to her apartment. She lived on the 4th floor, and the balcony of her apartment faced westward. I sprawled out on the couch, and she got me a few zip-bags of ice, which I strategically placed around my body.

A tabby cat crawled onto my chest as I lay on the couch. The kitty hovered over me, it's green eyes staring into mine. For a moment, I thought it was trying to steal my soul.

"That's Gizmo. Brush him off if he gets annoying."

He plopped down on my chest and began to purr.

"Do you need me to call anybody?" the girl asked.

"Yeah. Jack Donovan." I gave her the number, and she dialed Jack's phone while I kept the icepack on my face.

"He's not picking up. Do you want me to leave a message?"

"Yeah. Tell him Paxton caught up with me and to watch his back."

She relayed information, then ended the call. "Is there anybody else I should call?"

"Call Lyric Stone."

"You know Lyric Stone? I love her. She's so spunky. I watch her on the news all the time."

I gave her Lyric's number, and she called.

"Voicemail," the girl said a moment after dialing. "Do you want me to leave a message?"

I had forgotten for an instant that Lyric didn't have her cell phone with her. She was at the Château, but I didn't know what name she was staying under.

"Tell her I'm alive, and that's the important part. Sorry about the car."

"He says he's alive, and he's sorry about the car..." the girl repeated.

"Tell her I've run into some trouble and will catch up with her later and to stay put."

She relayed the rest of the message, then ended the call.

"What happened to the car?"

"She's going to kill me," I groaned. "I don't know what happened to it. It could still be on the side of the road, or it could have been impounded."

"What kind of car?"

"Ferrari."

She cringed. "You're in trouble."

"I know."

"Can I get you anything to drink?"

"Water would be great. Thank you." My lips were puffy and split, and I sounded like I had just gotten back from the dentist. I tongued all of my teeth, feeling the ridges of my molars. I still had them all, miraculously.

The girl brought me a glass of water and handed me two gel-caps of ibuprofen, even though I didn't ask for it. I took the capsules and swallowed them down.

"I really think you should go to the hospital. You could have a concussion. Are you having any double vision? Headache? Memory loss?"

"No, I feel fine," I lied. "Are you in the medical field?"

"No. But my older brother was a daredevil, and I made more than a few trips to the ER with him growing up."

"Tell me your name again?" I asked.

"Opal."

"That's a pretty name."

"Thank you. I hated it growing up. My older sister's name is Amethyst, and my younger sister's name is Ruby. My folks were kind of new-agey."

"Were?"

She frowned. "They were killed during a carjacking."

"I'm sorry to hear that."

She shrugged. "It happened when I was 16. That's life. You either deal with the crap that comes your way, or you get buried by it."

"Amen to that." I paused for a moment. "What's your brother's name?"

"Jasper." She sighed. "Lucky bastard. He got a normal-sounding name. But he still got teased a lot as a kid."

"Kids can be cruel," I said.

"Judging by the looks of you, so can adults."

"All things considered, I caught a lucky break."

"If you call this lucky, I'd hate to see your version of bad luck."

I started to chuckle but stopped myself before the pain in my ribs grew too intense.

"Can you tell me what you were doing undercover?"

I gave her a hesitant look through my swollen eyes.

"Just tell me to leave you alone if I'm bothering you. I'm inquisitive, and I like to ask a lot of questions. I'm an aspiring screenwriter. I study film at USC. So, this kind of thing is fascinating to me. You probably can't say anything about ongoing investigations. Top-secret and all that stuff, right?"

I gave her the short version of everything.

Her eyes rounded, and she stared at me in disbelief. "You need to tell someone!"

"I don't know how deep Paxton's connections go. As far as he knows, I'm dead right now. And that's the way I like it. Gives me the advantage of surprise."

"I know someone who can help."

I arched a curious eyebrow.

40

"My brother is a deputy district attorney," Opal said. "He can help you."

I looked at her with cautious optimism.

"And I know you can trust him." She grabbed her phone and dialed the number before I could protest.

A groggy voice answered the other end of the line. It was well past midnight.

"Hey, it's me."

Her brother grumbled something, and it didn't sound too pleasant.

"Yes, I know what time it is," Opal said. "This is important."

The voice crackled through the speaker of her phone.

"You're not going to believe what I'm about to tell you," Opal said.

She gave him an even shorter version of my story. They

talked for a few minutes, then she handed the phone to me. I put the device to my ear and said hello.

"That's a pretty tall tale you're telling," Jasper said. "Do you have any proof to back it up?"

"No," I said reluctantly. "Other than an eyewitness that can put Detective Paxton at the Château the night Mia drowned, and a former prostitute that will testify Paxton blackmailed her and demanded sexual favors. One of Nikki Griffin's girls."

Jasper scoffed. "A former prostitute? What's her name?"

"Can't say."

"Okay. Let me tell you how it is. You don't have shit. Defense counsel will tear through the hooker and discredit her immediately. I'll bet you dollars to donuts she's got priors, and probably a drug conviction. Am I right? And you expect the jury to believe her testimony against that of a decorated detective with an outstanding record?"

"Like I said. I don't have anything substantial."

He paused for a moment. "You know what I think... I think my sister's overly compassionate heart brought in a stray crazy person. And quite frankly, I'm concerned for her safety with you in her apartment. I'm tempted to call the police and send a unit over right now."

"You're not going to do that," I said.

"Why not?"

"Because there's a part of you that knows I am telling the truth. Otherwise, you wouldn't still be on the phone."

"Call it a courtesy to my naïve little sister."

I told him to call Sheriff Daniels and call me back. I ended the call and handed the device back to Opal.

She looked at me with curious eyes. "What did he say?"

I told her.

She huffed. "What a jackass. And I am not naïve!"

Jasper called back a few minutes later. Opal answered, then after a brief exchange, "He wants to talk to you."

She handed me the phone.

"Do my credentials check out?"

He didn't answer directly, but his continuation of the conversation was an unspoken *yes*. "I want to help you, I really do. But you need to help me. Tomorrow, I'll meet you down at the Office of the Inspector General. You can fill out a complaint, and we can start a formal investigation."

"No. Too risky."

"I can guarantee we have oversight in place specifically to investigate these types of criminal allegations against police officers."

"And I'm telling you I just got beaten within an inch of my life at the behest of two of LA's finest. You'll forgive me if I don't put a lot of faith in your system."

He sighed. "Look, you can go online and fill out an anonymous complaint. But without any substantial evidence, nothing will come of it. If you do want to make a statement, we may be able to get Paxton on assault, kidnapping, and a host of other charges."

It would be my word against Paxton's and his partners. I couldn't see much happening from a formal complaint without indisputable evidence. I didn't know the structure of the department here. Oftentimes, IA divisions are in the same building and under the same command structure as the rest of the department. Asking cops to police themselves was like asking burglars to stand neighborhood watch. People look out for their own. It's just human nature. No cop wants to turn on another cop.

In my experience, 99% of cops are honest, hard-working people who put up with an inordinate amount of shit in an attempt to make the world a better place. But Paxton and his group of bad apples were making the whole organization seem rotten. Sorting out who to trust was impossible.

"I appreciate your time," I said. "I'll think about it."

I handed the phone back to Opal.

Chuck Paxton had pissed me off, and I was seriously considering taking care of this the clean and simple way.

I had made a resolution not to use deadly force unless absolutely justified. I wasn't an assassin. Not anymore. My brain was jumping through mental hoops trying to make the use of force in this situation seem justified.

In a way, it was justified.

Paxton was a dirt-ball, and he would keep abusing his position of authority until somebody stopped him. The world would be a better place without him. No doubt, some other scumbag would step up to take his place, but that wasn't an excuse to let him continue. All it takes for evil to flourish is for good men to do nothing.

But I had made a promise to myself and to the Universe—I wasn't inclined to break it.

I'd been given a second chance at life, and I needed to stay as squeaky clean as possible. As much as I wanted to find Paxton and kill him in cold blood, I wasn't going to do that. But it sure was tempting.

41

I crashed on Opal's couch and woke up in the morning with Gizmo purring beside me. Everything hurt. I felt 907 years old.

The morning sun filtered through the blinds, and I attempted to peel myself from the couch. It was a slow, painful process. I staggered to the guest bathroom and caught a glimpse of my face. I had black circles under both my eyes. My face was puffy, swollen, and discolored. My arms, legs, and chest were multiple shades of purple, blue, green, and yellow. I looked like a horror show.

Afterward, I hobbled to the kitchen and pulled open the fridge. I grabbed a bottle of water, twisted the top, and guzzled it down. My mouth was sand.

Opal emerged from the bedroom, wearing a T-shirt and men's boxers.

"I hope you don't mind," I said, lifting up the bottle of water.

"Help yourself." She wiped the sleep from her eyes. She

almost cringed when she saw my condition. "How are you feeling?"

"Like I got run over by a steamroller."

She didn't have a landline. Just a cell phone.

"You mind if I use your phone to call a cab?" I asked.

"Where do you need to go?"

"Back to the Château."

"I can take you."

"Are you sure?"

"It's not a big deal. I don't have class till later."

"You didn't hear back from anyone we called last night, did you?"

"I have my phone on *do not disturb* at night. Let me go check." She slipped back into the bedroom and emerged a moment later, holding her smartphone. She shook her head. "Nope. No calls."

My brow knitted together. It was early in the morning, and I figured JD was probably still asleep. The band had probably tied one on last night. Lyric didn't have her phone, so it made sense she never got my message.

"Tell me what you want, and I'll cook you breakfast," I said.

"You don't have to do that."

"It's the least I can do in return for your hospitality.

She gave me a doubtful glance. "Are you sure you're healthy enough to fix breakfast?"

I frowned at her, playfully. It hurt to frown. I made a mental note not to do it again.

"I'm going to slip into the shower while you make breakfast."

She disappeared back into the bedroom and closed the door. A moment later, I heard the shower nozzle twist and the water spray across the tile.

I sifted through the fridge and found eggs, bacon, cheese, ham, and spinach. I grilled up omelettes and bacon, and we had a nice breakfast. I was thankful I still had my teeth and could chew. Sipping your food through a straw with a broken jaw is no fun. I tried to be thankful for what I *did* have, and not regretful over what I didn't.

After breakfast, I asked her if she had a hat and sunglasses I could borrow. She dug through her closet and found a ball cap and handed me a pair of women's oversized sunglasses. I tried them on, and they were a little too narrow for my face but better than nothing. I looked ridiculous. But this was Hollywood, I would fit right in. And hopefully, the disguise would somewhat conceal my identity.

She locked her apartment as we left, and we ambled to the parking garage. I tried not to limp but didn't do a very good job. I delicately climbed into the passenger seat of her Mini Cooper. It was low to the ground, and my legs and back hurt when I tried to stuff myself into the tiny car.

She dropped the top and pulled out of the garage. The wind swirled around the cabin, and the morning sun hovered in the air, casting warm rays of LA sunshine.

It was a nice day.

The sun had burned away the chaos of the night and concealed the ugly, dark side of the city.

We took the 10 west, then headed north on La Cienega. A few minutes later, we pulled into the secluded entrance to the Château.

"I can't thank you enough for coming to my aid."

"No problem. I would have wanted someone to do the same for me." She paused. "I really think you should consider making an official report like my brother suggested."

"I just don't know how much good it would do." I frowned.

"So, is this it? Will I ever see you again? I feel like I'm invested in your story now. I have to know if you get this guy."

"Let me see your phone," I said.

She handed the device to me, and I programmed in my number. I entered Joel's information as well.

"I've added my contact info as well as my agent's, Joel. He's with Inventive Artists Agency. One of the best in town. You're an aspiring screenwriter, right?"

She nodded, eagerly.

"Call Joel, tell him I referred you. I can't make any guarantees, but if your stuff is good, you never know."

"Thank you!" she said with bright eyes. "That's amazingly generous of you."

"Like I said, it's the least I could do."

"I'm a hugger. Give me a hug," she said.

I leaned across the center console, and I tried not to wince as she gave me a hug.

"Oops, sorry!" she said, seeing my pained face.

I climbed out of the car and stepped into the lobby. I strolled to the front desk and flashed my badge. "I'm looking for Lyric Stone. She checked in last night under an assumed name."

42

The clerk punched in the information and scanned the computer screen. She didn't say anything about my bruised face. I think the sunglasses concealed most of it. But my lips were fat, split, and swollen.

"I'm sorry, sir. But it seems like the guest you are inquiring about checked out this morning."

My brow lifted with surprise. What!?"

"I'm sorry, sir."

"You're sure?"

She checked the screen again. "Yes, sir. Positive."

I grumbled to myself, then said, "Thank you."

I left the desk and headed to the elevators. The call button lit up as I pressed it, and a moment later, the doors slid open. I made my way back to the hotel room and knocked on the door. I didn't have my key, and I had forgotten to get another one at the front desk. I didn't think about it until I dug my hand into my pocket for it.

Nobody answered.

I kept banging on the door.

Somebody finally shouted, "Go away! No service."

"It's Tyson. Open the door."

A moment later, I heard footsteps. Dizzy pulled open the door, and his jet black hair looked like a tornado hit it. Twisted strands hung in his face. His eyelids were heavy, and he could barely keep them open. "You look like you had a rougher night than we did."

I stepped into the foyer and marched past him.

"Nice shades," he said, genuinely impressed.

The hotel room was wrecked. Empty beer cans and whiskey bottles were strewn about. Naked girls were bunched like sardines into the foldout bed. It looked like the band had a hell of a good time last night. A lot better than I did.

I moved to the house phone and dialed Lyric's cell phone. It went straight to voicemail. "Hey, I'm back at the Château. The front desk said you checked out. Where are you? I don't have my cell phone any longer. Call me at the hotel. Let me know you're okay."

JD emerged from his bedroom. "What happened to you?"

I told him about my exploits. "Did you get my message?"

"Sorry, man. Things got pretty out of hand last night."

"I see that."

"I think we hit just about every club on the strip." He puffed up with a proud grin. "I behaved myself."

"Still saving yourself for Sloan?"

"I am. I'm born again."

I rolled my eyes, and even that hurt.

"When we finally hook up, it's gonna be so good," JD said, salivating at the possibility.

"I'm worried about Lyric," I said.

"Do you think she went back to her house?"

I shrugged. "She's not answering her phone. I don't know where she could be." I sighed. "I'm going to take a shower, get changed, then catch a cab to her place and see if she's there."

"Do you want me to go with you?"

I shook my head. "No. You don't need to get dragged into this."

He looked at me like I was crazy. "What you get dragged into, I get dragged into, brother."

A slight smirk curled my face. Good friends are priceless.

I took off my hat and sunglasses. JD's eyes rounded. "Damn, son, they worked you over good!"

"Tell me about it."

I crawled into the shower and let the warm water soothe my aching muscles. After toweling off, I got dressed—even that was a task. I knew from experience I needed to keep moving. Laying around would just cause things to stiffen up.

I stepped from the bedroom into the common area of the suite. The band was up, and Dizzy was on the balcony with one of the strippers. They were both smoking a joint. Half-naked girls bobbled around without a care in the world.

JD emerged from his bedroom with a pistol in a Kydex holster. He handed it to me. "I figure you could use this." I pulled the weapon from the holster, press-checked it, then affixed the holster inside my waistband.

He pulled out a wad of cash from his pocket and handed it to me. "A little walking-around money."

"I need a new phone, too. They took everything."

"We'll swing by Lyric's, then we can hit a store afterward and pick up a new device."

We left the band, headed down to the lobby, and caught a cab. The car climbed up into the hills, twisting through Lyric's neighborhood. When the driver dropped us off, I asked him to wait.

I hopped out of the car and scurried up the driveway and rang the front doorbell. There was no answer. No sign of forced entry.

I walked the perimeter of the house, looking for anything amiss. But there were no broken windows, no doors left ajar. Everything was locked up tight. I kept peering in through the windows, looking for Lyric. I was sure a neighbor would call the cops, thinking I was a peeping Tom.

The cab driver was still parked in front of the house after we had trekked around the premises. We climbed into the car, and I told him to take us to the nearest mall.

We wandered through the mall in Century City and found the *Pear* store. JD put my new phone on his credit card. I immediately synced the device with the cloud and downloaded my contacts. Then I remotely erased my old phone and locked it out.

There were no messages or calls from Lyric. I was seriously worried at this point in time.

We left the mall and caught a cab back to the Château. The room smelled like a medical marijuana dispensary when we entered, and a bluish haze filled the air.

"Dude, glad you made it back. We got soundcheck in an hour." Dizzy said.

Jack's eyes rounded. "Shit, I forgot."

"How could you forget. It's the entire reason we came out here."

All of the band's gear was still in the van. They needed to take it to the venue, load in, set up for soundcheck, then break it down again, only to set it up later for the show. Each band that evening would have half an hour, then they were kicked off stage. It was a high-churn venue, and they were all paying for the privilege to grace the infamous stage.

I needed to get off my feet for a minute. I was so battered and bruised that I was already worn out, and I hadn't done anything yet. I crawled into bed with the intention of just laying down for a few minutes, but I must have dozed off.

When I woke up, the band was gone. The TV in the living room was still on, tuned to a local channel. I staggered into the living room, brushed some of the beer cans off the sofa, and took a seat.

My bones creaked.

A reporter came on TV with a breaking news segment. "One of KXTLA's own is missing. We bring you concerning news this afternoon that investigative reporter, Lyric Stone, is currently missing. She failed to show up at the studio today, and her car was found abandoned near Olympic. Station management has been unable to reach her. If anyone has seen her, or has information about her whereabouts, please contact the station or local law enforcement immediately. We will continue to keep you updated on this concerning development."

43

M y stomach twisted, and my hands balled into fists. I grit my teeth and grumbled a few obscenities.

There was no doubt who was responsible, but I felt helpless.

I called Isabella. "I have a situation."

"What else is new?"

I gave her the details. "Can you track Chuck Paxton's cell phone and tell me where he is?"

"I can try."

"Find Lyric Stone's cell phone for me as well."

"I'll call you back."

I ended the call and waited on the edge of my seat like a teenage girl waiting for someone to ask her to prom. I climbed off the couch and paced the room, nervous sweat misting my skin. Isabella couldn't call me back fast enough.

I swiped the screen and answered the phone when it rang. "What did you find out?"

"The number I have for Paxton is not showing up on the grid. He could be using a burner phone, or it could be turned off."

"What about Lyric?"

"From what I can tell, her phone is at her house in the hills."

I grimaced. "She's not there. I checked earlier. The news has reported her missing."

"What do you want me to do?" Isabella asked. It was a genuine offer, and something she rarely volunteered.

I noticed that she had stopped holding her services over my head. I knew the time would come when she would ask for a return favor, but she wasn't as vocal about it anymore. Perhaps it was an implied part of our communication. Perhaps she appreciated what I had done for her in Colombia.

"Let me know if Paxton pops up on your radar."

"Will do," she said.

I ended the call and slipped my phone back into my pocket.

In my mind, I ran through the possibilities. Either Paxton had taken Lyric hostage, or he had killed her. I hated to admit it, but my mind gravitated toward the latter. For all Paxton knew, I was dead. What good would taking Lyric as a hostage serve unless he knew I was still alive? And if that was the case, why wouldn't he just come after me directly?

I kept pacing around the hotel room as the wheels spun in

my mind. After another 20 minutes of frantic worry, my phone buzzed again. I pulled the device from my pocket and looked at the screen. It was Nikki Griffin. I took the call.

"Deputy Wild?" Nikki's sultry, but commanding voice asked.

"I'm surprised you called," I said.

"Desperate times call for desperate measures."

"I spoke with Bonnie."

"I know. That's why I'm calling. I am as tired of a certain detective as you are, Deputy."

"Have you been watching the news? I think he may have done something to Lyric?"

"In my experience, Detective Paxton is capable of just about anything. I have been living under his thumb for far too long. Bonnie had enough, and I think she was finally ready to file a formal complaint. That's what has me worried. I can't get in touch with her."

My heart sank, and I clenched my jaw.

"I thought she'd be safe on my boat," Nikki said. "I'm worried sick, and I feel terrible. Bonnie is like a little sister to me."

A little sister that she pimps out on occasion.

"Do you think you could meet me down at the marina to check on her?"

44

I sent JD a text that I was heading down to the marina. I didn't hear back. I figured he was in the middle of the soundcheck.

Joel called. "I've got a meeting set up with Susan Monday morning. 9 AM. I spoke with David, he's really excited. He says you two are in sync creatively, and he has high hopes for the series."

"That's great. I'm about to run out the door. Can I call you later?"

"Sure. One thing. I got a call from a girl named Opal... Says you referred her?"

"Yeah."

"Did you have a chance to read her writing? Is she any good?"

"No. I didn't read anything. She did me a favor."

"Gotcha," he replied, almost with a groan.

"A big favor."

"Was the blow job that good?"

"Not that kind of favor."

I gave him the condensed version of what happened.

"Are you okay?"

"I'm fine. A little battered and bruised, but I'm fine."

"Geez, Tyson. All you had to do was come out here and work on a story with the biggest director in Hollywood. Can't you go one minute without getting yourself into trouble?"

"I try to keep things interesting," I said. "And it keeps you employed."

"I have plenty of other clients. I don't need you to get beaten half to death just to have a story to sell."

"Is that genuine concern I hear in your voice?" I asked.

"Do you even need to ask?"

I chuckled. "You're one-of-a-kind, Joel. Especially in this town."

"I will take that as a compliment." He paused. "Try to stay out of trouble," he said, knowing that was impossible.

Just as I hung up, there was a knock at the door.

A spike of concern jolted through me. There was no doubt I was unsettled and a little twitchy after what I had been through.

My hands snatched the pistol from its holster, and I crept down the foyer to the door. I peered through the tiny peephole. Through the distorted lens, I saw a stunning brunette with a roller case in tow.

My brow crinkled with shock.

It was Sloan.

I jammed the pistol back into the holster, unlatched the door, and pulled it open.

"Surprise!" she said with a cheery smile. The cheery smile instantly faded. "My God, what happened to your face?"

"Oh, it's nothing. Tripped and fell."

She gave me a skeptical glance.

"What are you doing here?" I asked, surprised to see her.

Concern washed over her pretty face. "Should I not have come?"

"Quite the contrary. I think JD will be ecstatic to see you." I stepped aside and motioned for her to enter.

"I should have told him I was coming." She rolled her bag into the suite, and the flowery scent of her perfume filled the air.

I poked my head into the exterior hallway and scanned both directions.

It was empty.

I closed the door and followed her into the living room. "JD will be delighted."

Sloan's lip curled with disgust. The place looked like a shithole.

"I can see you guys are having fun."

I'm sure she noticed a pair of frilly panties on the floor by the pull out sofa-bed. "Delighted, huh?"

"Don't worry. Jack's not having *that* much fun."

She rolled her eyes, knowing Jack's predilections. "Where is everybody?"

"They're at the soundcheck."

"I thought I'd come out for the show. Lend a little moral support. Doesn't look like they need it."

"Trust me. Jack will be over the moon to see you. He hasn't stopped talking about you since we got here."

She tried to hide a smirk.

"Listen, I've got to run. Make yourself at home." I pointed to Jack's bedroom. "That's where Jack is sleeping. I'm sure he won't mind if you take up residence there."

She arched a sassy eyebrow at me. "He's not getting that lucky."

I raised my hands instantly. "What happens between y'all is between y'all."

"He's at *Sour Mash*, right?"

I nodded. "It's just a few blocks down the street if you want to walk."

"I might do that after I settle in."

I told her I'd see her later, then left the hotel room, made my way down to the lobby, and caught a traditional cab to the marina.

I turned off my phone. Call me paranoid, but I didn't want anyone tracking or tracing my movements.

The amber ball hovered over the horizon, sparkling the water as we pulled into the parking lot of the marina. Boats gently swayed in their slips, and seabirds hovered in the draft. I surveyed the parking lot before stepping out of the cab. The lot was half full with vehicles. I didn't see anything unusual.

I paid the driver in cash, then stepped out of the car. The driver sped away.

My eyes scanned the lot for Nikki, but I didn't see her. Maybe she was waiting for me on the boat.

45

Waves lapped against the hull of the *Nauti-Gal*. I ambled down the dock, scanning the area. I stepped through the boarding gate into the cockpit, then advanced to the sliding glass doors of the salon. My palm was placed firmly against the grip of my pistol.

The salon was empty.

With a gentle tug, I slid the door open. "Nikki? Bonnie?"

There was no reply.

I drew my pistol and advanced forward. Through the front windows, I could see the bow—it was empty. I hadn't seen anyone on the flybridge as I approached.

"Is anyone here?"

The boat creaked and groaned as it gently swayed.

I descended the steps, heading below deck. I poked my head into the companionway and surveyed both directions. I called out for Nikki and Bonnie again, but there was no response.

I inched forward and cautiously opened the hatch to the guest stateroom. The barrel of my pistol panned across the compartment. It was empty.

I pulled the hatch shut and continued aft to the master stateroom. I gripped the handle and twisted the hatch open, pushing into the compartment with my weapon ready to neutralize any threats.

Bonnie lay on the bed, pale and lifeless. From the bruising around her neck, it looked like she'd been strangled.

My heart sank, and a grimace tugged my face. I pushed into the compartment and checked for vitals, but I knew she was long gone. Her skin was cold to the touch.

By the time I turned back to the hatch, I was greeted by the daunting barrel of a black semi-automatic pistol, firmly gripped by Paxton's sleazy hand. He had crept down the companionway while I was preoccupied with Bonnie's corpse.

"So glad you could join us, Deputy Wild," Paxton said. "Put your weapon on the deck and slide it toward me."

I complied.

His partner, Duke, hovered behind him.

Paxton kept his weapon aimed at me as he knelt down and picked up the gun.

"That gun is a loner, so if I could have it back at the end of this, I'd appreciate it."

Paxton chuckled. "You know, it's a shame. I kind of like you. You're funny. But I think you've used up all your lives. Judging by the looks of you, Hector and his boys worked you over pretty good. But not good enough. I will have a long talk with Hector, believe me."

Paxton tossed me a pair of handcuffs.

There was a sconce light bolted to the bulkhead. It had a double stem, L-shaped arm. I slapped one cuff around my wrist, then threaded the other through the arms of the lamp and ratcheted it tight. I figured with some doing, I might be able to pry the whole thing loose from the bulkhead.

"Where's Lyric?" I asked.

"I don't know why you bother asking questions at this point. Where you are going, the answers won't do you any good."

He took my phone before he pulled the hatch shut. I heard his footsteps shuffle across the deck, then up the stairs to the salon.

I tugged on the sconce, trying to pry it from the bulkhead. It felt solid. It would take a lot more effort than I anticipated.

A few minutes later, the engines rumbled to life, and soon we were idling out of the marina.

It was a troublesome development.

Bonnie's body was sprawled out on the bed. There was a bobby-pin in her hair. In the commotion of her death, and struggle for life, her hair had been tousled and the pin barely clung to a nodded tangle of hair. If I could reach it, I might be able to pick the lock to the handcuff.

I stretched for the bed, angling from the sconce. The bobby-pin was just out of reach.

I grabbed the sheets and pulled the body closer. With a few more tugs, the metal pin was within reach. I snatched it between my fingers, spread the clip, and inserted it into the key slot. It only took a few seconds of fumbling with the mechanism, and the cuff released. I pulled my wrist free and glanced around the compartment, looking for anything I could use as a weapon.

I rifled through the drawers in the stateroom but found nothing besides frilly lace panties, jewelry, clothing, a baseball cap, sunglasses, and other personal belongings—some of which were quite naughty. This was Nikki's stateroom, after all.

I padded across the compartment to the hatch and listened. The engine rumbled, and the boat pitched as it carved through the swells. Through the porthole, I could see the marina in the distance. We were heading out to the open ocean. There was no doubt that Paxton planned to kill me and dump me overboard, along with Bonnie's body.

I slowly twisted the handle and pulled the hatch open without making a sound. I tiptoed into the companionway and pulled the hatch shut behind me. Moving forward, I held up at the bulkhead near the stairs to the salon.

Paxton's voice filtered below deck. He was talking with his partner. "Go check on our guest. Make sure he is not getting into any trouble."

46

I darted into the guest suite across the corridor and pulled the hatch shut behind me.

Duke's heavy footsteps pounded down the stairs, then he headed aft to the master stateroom.

I quietly pushed out of the guest compartment and crept aft. Just as Duke swung open the hatch to the master stateroom, I kicked the back of his knee. His legs buckled, dropping him to the deck. I planted a hard knee into his spine, then dropped an elbow onto his neck, causing him to tumble forward on all fours. I cocked my foot back and kicked him in the balls as hard as I could.

He groaned in agony, flattening to the deck. I pounced on his back and put him in a choke hold. I squeezed my arm tight, and he clawed at me.

Duke was a big guy, and I felt like I was trying to strangle an ox. He pushed off the deck and rolled onto his back. I held on for dear life, crunching under the weight of the massive beast. My already cracked ribs sent a jolt of pain through my body.

I mustered all the strength I had, trying to choke the life out of the bastard. He kept elbowing me in the ribs and clawing at me. He reached a meaty hand back, grabbed a tuft of my hair, and pulled as hard as he could. He torqued my neck, and I felt like the follicles were going to rip from my scalp if this continued much longer.

He reached for his pistol and drew it from its holster. He brought the weapon around, angling it behind him at my face. His thumb fumbled to click off the safety.

I kept squeezing tight, cutting off the blood flow to his brain. The gun hovered there for a second, drawing closer. Then Duke went limp, and the gun clattered to the deck. The big ogre melted like warm putty.

He was like a fallen sequoia on top of me, pinning me to the deck. Not a place I wanted to be. The guy weighed a ton.

With my left hand, I fumbled for the pistol on the deck and tried to shove the ogre off of me.

Paxton cut the throttle, and the boat settled into the swells. I guess Paxton had heard the commotion and made his way below deck to investigate. He pushed into the compartment with his weapon drawn just as I picked up Duke's pistol.

There was no time for witty banter. No condescending exchanges. Paxton squeezed the trigger.

So did I.

I wasn't naturally left-handed, but I had acquired the ability to shoot either way, though I was better right-handed.

The pistol hammered against my palm, and muzzle flash flickered from the barrel. Our bullets crisscrossed in the air, and the sharp smell of gunpowder wafted through the compartment.

I heard a dull thud and felt a jolt to my chest. That typically wasn't a good sign.

My bullet hit Paxton in the chest, spewing a geyser of crimson blood as he fell back against the bulkhead, then slid to the deck.

I squeezed another shot off, pelting him for a second time in the chest, splattering the bulkhead red.

Paxton stared at me for a moment with bewildered eyes. He attempted to fire one last shot, but he could barely keep his pistol raised. His strength faded, and so did his essence.

The gun clattered to the deck as it fell from his hand, and Paxton's body went limp.

The bullet he shot at me had entered Duke's chest, and the big meaty ogre absorbed the impact, shielding me from the blast.

I crawled out from underneath the dead slab of meat and felt my chest for any penetrating wounds.

I'd gotten lucky.

I checked both of the stiffs, just to make sure they were dead. I searched Paxton and found JD's pistol. I took it back and shoved it into the holster in my waistband. I retrieved my new phone. With my shirt, I wiped down Duke's pistol, removing my fingerprints, then carefully placed it into his hand and made sure to put his prints on the weapon and on the trigger. I found the handcuffs and wiped my prints from the metal. There were three corpses on this boat, and I had no intention of reporting the incident to the LAPD.

I left the stateroom, wiped my prints from the door handle, and continued down the companionway, wiping any surfaces I had touched.

I climbed the stairs to the salon and surveyed the area. There was no one else on board, and the boat was drifting through the water a few miles offshore. The sun had dipped over the horizon, and the sky was midnight blue—the last traces of light keeping it from total blackness.

At the helm, I throttled up and banked the boat around, heading back to the marina. The engines rumbled, and the yacht plowed through the swells.

47

The boat idled through the inky water of the marina, and I pulled into the slip and tied off. There was no reason to connect water and power. I wiped down the helm controls and anything else I might have touched. I remembered there was a baseball cap in one of the drawers in the master stateroom. I grabbed the hat and a pair of sunglasses before leaving the yacht.

I stepped to the aft deck, pushed through the boarding gate, and onto the dock. The night sky had a purple-ish glow from the lights of the city, making it impossible to see any stars overhead.

I walked away from the yacht casually. There was no one else in this section of the marina. Before long, I was strolling across the dark parking lot. My phone was off, and I didn't have any intention of turning it on. I didn't want phone records to show I was anywhere near this place.

I kept walking. My body was sore and achy, but adrenaline still pumped through my veins from the ordeal. I wasn't quite sure how far it was from Marina del Rey to West Hollywood, but it was a lot farther than I wanted to walk.

At a corner gas station, I saw a cab filling up. I approached the driver. "Need a lift to West Hollywood."

"Hop in," the driver said.

I pulled open the door and slipped into the backseat. He finished pumping the gas, replaced the nozzle and gas cap, then climbed behind the wheel. He started up the car and switched on the meter. I watched the red numbers increase as we drove up the 405 and took the 10 to La Cienega.

During the drive, I had a sour, nervous feeling in my stomach. I had no idea what happened to Lyric—and with Paxton's demise, I would probably never know.

I had the cab driver drop me off at the corner of La Cienega and Sunset. I paid him in cash. I stepped to the curb and watched him drive away. He turned onto Sunset, heading east.

It was only a few blocks up to the Château. I staggered into the lobby, and requested another key from the front desk. I marched to the elevators and went up to my suite. Through the door, I heard commotion inside. I slipped my key into the slot, pushed open the door, and stepped into the foyer.

JD and the crew were pre-gaming before the show.

Jack's face twisted when he saw me. "What the hell happened to you?"

"We don't have a dirty cop problem anymore," I said.

"I gotta hear this."

I dug in my pocket and pulled out my cell phone. I powered the device on, and an instant later, a dozen texts dinged through, flashing on my screen.

Most of them were from JD.

But a few were from Lyric.

I called her back immediately. "Where are you?"

"I was about to ask you the same thing. I've been trying to get in touch with you all afternoon."

"I was worried sick about you. They said you were missing on the news. The hotel said you checked out, and you weren't at home."

"Oh, I have to check in with you now?" she asked in a sassy, playful tone. "I'm still at the Château, silly."

"They said you checked out."

"I told them at the front desk not to tell anyone that I was here, and that if a cop came looking for me, tell him I checked out."

I exhaled a breath, chuckling at my stupidity. "I didn't consider that."

"I forgot to call into the station, and since I didn't have my cell phone, they thought the worst. Especially after all the threats and vandalism I've been experiencing lately."

"I'm glad you're okay."

"I have to admit, I was getting worried about you."

"I'm fine. Sort of. But, I think our situation is taken care of. I'll tell you all about it later."

"What about my car?"

I cringed. "Sorry about that."

"I haven't been inclined to call the LAPD and inquire about it. Do I even want to know?"

I gave her the full story and didn't spare any details. She seemed understanding.

"Look, I'm going to hop in the shower. It's been a rough few days. JD's band is playing tonight. You should tag along if you're up to it."

"Are you kidding me? I've been cooped up in this hotel room all day, stressed out of my mind. The only time I left was to get my phone from the house. I need a little release."

I gave her my room number and told her to come by when she was ready.

I went to the bathroom and peeled out of my clothes. My dress shirt was speckled with blood. I soaked it in the sink, trying to get the stains out of it before I sent it out to be cleaned.

I twisted the nozzle and, when the shower was steaming, climbed inside and let the water soothe my aching muscles. Afterward, I got dressed and prepared myself for a much-needed drink.

I rejoined the others in the living room.

"Can you believe who showed up?" JD asked, a proud grin on his face.

Sloan smiled. "I couldn't miss your big debut in Hollywood."

"I'm really glad you're here. This moment wouldn't be the same without someone special to share it with."

She mocked him, playfully. "Aw, isn't that sweet?"

"It *is* sweet, if I do say so myself," JD said. He looked at his watch. "We need to get going. Don't want to miss our own show. Scarlett's running late, but she said she'd meet us there."

There was a knock at the door. When I pulled it open, Lyric's eyes widened. "Oh, my God! What happened to your face?"

"I'll tell you all about it." I motioned for her to enter.

Lyric sauntered into the living room, wearing a tight black dress and stiletto heels. I introduced her to the gang, and in typical fashion, they drooled.

The two bottles of whiskey that I bought from the liquor store were tapped out, and the band had gone through everything in the minibar. It would be an expensive bill, but the studio was picking up the tab. I'm sure they were used to Hollywood excesses.

We left the hotel and walked several blocks west to *Sour Mash*. The bouncer recognized Jack from the soundcheck and waved us in. I think he had realized he wasn't the famous '80s singer. The place was packed, and there was a line around the corner to get in. I think even JD was stunned by the size of the crowd.

"I knew we sold out, but I didn't expect this many people," JD said.

Another band was on stage, cranking out solid rock 'n' roll.

The deafening wave of sound blanketed the audience. The place smelled like spilled beer and whiskey, mixed with recreational herbal spices.

Scarlett showed up with one of her hot friends—a stunning brunette with sparkling blue eyes, tanned skin, and legs for days.

The band ogled the two and crowded around them. JD scowled at his bandmates, flashing them threatening glances.

Scarlett could take care of herself. She'd been surrounded by ravenous wolves many times before.

Unlike the bars back home, the band didn't get free drinks here. JD bought a round for everyone, and we all toasted to the debut of *Wild Fury* on the Sunset Strip.

It wasn't long before JD and the band headed back to the greenroom to put their game faces on. They finally took the stage around 11:30 PM. With all of Jack's promotional efforts —the billboards, the radio spots, the social media ads, and their aggressive flyer campaign on Sunset Boulevard—the eager crowd anticipated a monumental show.

The pressure was on *Wild Fury* to deliver.

The initial response from the crowd was optimistic, but not overwhelming. None of them had ever heard *Wild Fury* live before, except a few diehard fans that had found clips of the band's concerts online.

Styxx sat behind a candy apple red drum set and clicked off the beat. Dizzy and Crash chimed in. The bass boomed, and Dizzy's guitar crunched razor-like riffs. The kick drum pounded, and the wall of sound bowled over the crowd.

Jack pranced around on stage, his long hair flowing. He flung his hair, grabbed the microphone, and screamed the first verse.

The band hit the audience with a classic '80s hit. Waves of sonic bliss washed over the audience, soothing any apprehension they might have had about the quality of the band.

With perfect pitch, Jack howled the vocals, and the crowd roared.

Lights swirled, slashing the air. Fog machines billowed smoke onto the stage, and once again, rock 'n' roll ruled the day.

Howls erupted after the first song, and the audience cheered.

"You want more, or have you had enough?" JD asked the crowd.

His question was met with unanimous response.

He grinned. "This is one of our own."

The band launched into one of their originals. By the time the first chorus rolled around, heads were banging.

A surprised look painted Scarlett's face. She shouted in my ear, "Holy shit! They're actually good."

I chuckled. "Your old man's got talent. Who knew?"

The band hammered out a set that left the audience ecstatic. There were screams and whistles. Cheers and chants for more. *Wild Fury* had lightning in a bottle, and they had unleashed it on the Sunset Strip. The set created addicts and expanded their tribe of loyal followers.

After the show, the band was swarmed with groupies. There were short skirts, high heels, push-up bras, teased hair, and ample amounts of eye-catching cleavage.

Somehow, JD managed to ignore all of the luscious temptations. He made a beeline for Sloan, she was the only one he had eyes for. She gave him a hug and a kiss on the cheek and told him, "That was amazing. Best show yet."

A proud grin curled on Jack's face. "This is only the beginning."

48

A slick man in a suit plowed through the crowd of groupies, making his way to JD. He was in his late 20s, dark hair, dark eyes, handsome features, well groomed, expensive watch. He handed a business card to JD and flashed a brilliant smile. "Amazing show. And when I say amazing, I mean A-MAZ-ING! And I don't use that term often. Jonathan Sullivan. *Auralogic Records*. It's a pleasure to meet you."

The two shook hands.

"Thank you," JD said. "Good to meet you as well."

"Has anyone ever told you you look exactly like..."

"All the time."

"I did a double-take when I first saw your billboard. How have I not heard of the band before?"

"We are not local."

Jonathan's brow lifted with surprise. "Not local? Yet, you managed to pack this place. That's no easy feat."

JD grinned. "Well, we have a certain appeal."

"And a lot of marketing savvy. I saw your billboards, I heard your interview on the radio. I had to admit. I was intrigued. You coordinated all this yourself?"

Jack nodded with pride.

"Amazing. Look, I don't want to take up too much of your time, you have some well-deserved celebrating to do. But I like your style. And your sound is amazing. The originals you played... Did you write those, or did you hire a songwriter?"

"We wrote those as a band," JD said.

"Amazing." There was that rarely used word of his again. "I see big possibilities for you guys. What you've been able to accomplish on your own is—"

"Amazing?" JD asked.

"Indeed. But just imagine what you could do with the full marketing potential of a major record label behind you. I think the time is right for rock 'n' roll to return. And you guys could herald in a new era. Everything old is new again, and that neo-retro vintage sound is making a comeback."

An optimistic grin tugged on JD's lips.

"I'll get out of your hair and let you enjoy the rest of the evening. Call my office Monday. I'd like to get together with the band and talk more about the possibilities. In the meantime, enjoy your evening. Your bar tab is on me, so enjoy yourselves."

There were howls of approval from the band.

Jonathan flashed another smile and shook hands with the gang, then disappeared into the crowd.

"You heard the man," JD said. "Drinks on Jonathan!"

There was another roar from the group.

We proceeded to drink our fill until the bar shut down. We all stumbled back toward the hotel. Though it was only a few blocks, it seemed like a monumental task, given our inebriated condition. On more than a few occasions, several members of the band tumbled onto the concrete with wobbly steps. With a horde of groupies in tow, we packed into the hotel room, and the party continued until the wee hours of the morning.

It didn't take long for JD and Sloan to disappear into his bedroom. I had never seen him get much more than a peck on the cheek from her, so I was quite anxious to get a full report in the morning.

Lyric and I left the group to their debauchery and retired to my bedroom. I was battered and bruised, but I still managed to have a good time. Lyric went relatively easy on me. She got a little carried away at times, but I didn't mind her attempt to play rodeo queen.

In the morning, I got a call from Jasper, the deputy district attorney, just as the shafts of morning sun spilled through the blinds. "I thought you'd be interested to know that Detective Paxton was found dead on Nikki Griffin's boat in the marina, along with his partner. You wouldn't happen to know anything about that, would you?"

"That's news to me. Such a shame."

"Looks like he may have gotten into an altercation with his partner. It appears they shot each other. One of Nikki's girls, Bonnie Broussard, was found as well."

"Any word from Nikki?"

"LA County interviewed her. She claimed to know nothing about it. Has an alibi. Internal Affairs has launched a full investigation. I just thought you'd like to know."

I could tell by his tone of voice he knew I was holding something back, but he didn't press the issue.

I thanked him again for his offer to help, though he didn't do anything. Before he hung up, he thanked me for setting Opal up with my agent.

I texted Nikki Griffin: [You set me up.]

A moment later: *[Sorry. I had no choice. Glad to know you survived.]*

I left it at that. There was no doubt Paxton had threatened her.

After spending another hour rolling around the sheets with Lyric, I finally pulled myself out of bed, took a shower, then ordered room service.

When I staggered into the living area, the place was an indescribable wreck. The pullout bed was full of half-naked groupies. Beer cans, whiskey bottles, and bongs were scattered about. Dizzy had managed to score the pullout bed, while Styxx and Crash slept in sleeping bags on the floor— sleeping bags filled with groupies. Apparently, the guys played rock-paper-scissors for the privilege of sleeping in the bed each night.

I stepped onto the balcony and took a breath of morning air. I looked down at the pool where Mia Sophia had drowned. I gave her mother a call and filled her in on all the details. Nothing would bring her daughter back, but in some way, justice had been served. Paxton wouldn't be able to take advantage of anyone else. But power never leaves a void for long. Someone else would take his place, I was sure of it.

Sheriff Daniels called just as I was finishing up with Mia's mother. We said our goodbyes, and I clicked over to speak with the sheriff.

"I need you two dipshits back in Coconut Key immediately."

"Why? What's going on?"

"Nothing good. That's for sure."

JD stepped out of his bedroom with an ear-to-ear grin. I couldn't wait to hear about his adventure with Sloan.

His grin faded when he saw my face. He knew exactly who I was talking to by my expression. A heavy sigh escaped his lips, and he shook his head.

We still had business to take care of with the studio on Monday, and there was Jack's potential meeting with the record label. Something told me Sheriff Daniels wouldn't be too keen on us staying in LA for a few more days.

Ready for more?

The adventure continues with <u>Wild High</u>.

Join my <u>newsletter</u> *and find out what happens next!*

AUTHOR'S NOTE

Thanks for all the great reviews!

I've got more adventures for Tyson and JD. Stay tuned.

If you liked this book, let me know with a review on Amazon.

Hope you are well during this challenging time. Thanks for reading!

—*Tripp*

TYSON WILD

MAX MARS

The Orion Conspiracy

Blade of Vengeance

The Zero Code

Edge of the Abyss

Siege on Star Cruise 239

Phantom Corps

The Auriga Incident

Devastator

CONNECT WITH ME

I'm just a geek who loves to write. Follow me on Facebook.

www.trippellis.com

Made in the USA
Las Vegas, NV
09 November 2021

34055922R00163